In Flame

GAYE HİÇYILMAZ

In Flame

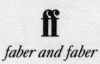

faber and faber

First published in 2000
by Faber and Faber Limited
3 Queen Square London WC1N 3AU

Typeset by Faber and Faber
Printed in England by Mackays of Chatham plc, Chatham, Kent

© Gaye Hiçyılmaz, 2000

Gaye Hiçyılmaz is hereby identified as author of this
work in accordance with Section 77 of the Copyright,
Designs and Patents Act 1988

A CIP record for this book
is available from the British Library

ISBN 0–571–20278–0

2 4 6 8 10 9 7 5 3 1

Chapter 1

'Of course,' Gran sighs, licking carefully, 'summer is not the same. Not now. Not any longer the same.' She sighs and licks again and wipes a drip of melted ice-cream from her soft, pink chin. She's missed another on her throat, but she's old now. And it is a blazing hot day. My jeans have stuck to me like a second, heavier skin. Mum and I don't say anything, not even when another blob slithers down on to her new blouse. I look away. Gran licks and sighs again.

Then Mum sighs too. She draws in a long breath and holds it, so that her face reddens. Then she sighs noisily. I assume that she's irritated by the mess, but I'm wrong. It's something else altogether.

'Anna!' Mum says sharply, not looking at the soiled blouse. 'Don't! Please?'

I glance up. Gran is so surprised by the reprimand that she forgets to lick. She stares open mouthed, tongue poised. Another lump begins its slide from the cone. This time she notices because it falls into her lap. As she flails around, searching for her hankie, she flicks off a small, round chocolatey blob which lands on Dad's nose. He rubs but misses the spot. Luke, who's nibbled down to the end of his cornet, begins to giggle. Then he chokes on a crumb.

Gran purses her lips and frowns. 'I can't help it, you know,' she says, in her shrivelling, trembly voice that is still strongly accented. 'I can't help being old. And I never wanted this cornet, did I? I said "no thank you" when Juliet asked. But nobody listened. I knew this was going to happen.

1

I didn't want ice-cream. This is what comes from your eating all the time: eating in the streets, eating round your television, eating as if any of you has ever been hungry.' She scowls, as her eyes settle on me. 'And if you don't watch out, Helen, you will be getting that ice-cream all over your . . . your . . .' She's eyeing my crop top. She's forgotten its name again, and never approved of it anyway. She says it makes me look like a hussy! If only! I'm just not the hussy type, not with my huge bosom and too grown-up face. Anyway, hussies have got guts.

But I'm sorry for her. It can't be any fun to be thrown into a disapproving tizz by the sight of your granddaughter's navel. Maybe it's a good thing I haven't had a piercing done. I'd never hear the end of that.

Luke is sniggering, so I flash him a warning glance. He shuts up instantly. He usually does. He's a sweet kid and very grown-up for seven. He and I rearrange our faces and smile expectantly at Gran. We're waiting for her 'summer is not the same' speech. She makes it so often that I've almost forgotten that it's not true. Luke, poor lamb, has grown up with them, because he was born after it happened. He believes her, and doesn't know any better.

But Mum does.

'For heaven's sake!' Mum spits her words out like pips. 'For heaven's sake, Anna, don't start on all that *now*!' Her voice is rising and I don't want to hear this.

Suddenly, on this beautiful day, with this beautiful view, stretching out before us, I want to be back in our old home in dirty, grey suburbia. I know that this new house is supposed to be home now, or that's what everybody keeps saying. But it isn't home for me. Not if I'm honest. I'd give anything to be back in the grotty old bedroom which I shared with the hot water tank. It was more cupboard than bedroom but I liked it. Staying on in that house might have been driving everybody else mad, but not me. I was happy there. It was so cramped that I kept my clothes in banana boxes and when friends came round they had to sit in a straight line on my bed, but I was happy. Despite everything and even afterwards, I was happy there. But I never said.

It's different for Luke. He's settled in already and is as happy as can be. It's like that for little kids, isn't it? They can change homes and schools easily because they soon forget.

And I never said that sometimes, when I was absolutely sure that nobody else was in the house, I'd untie the blind in Tom's old room and let it ride up in a puff of dust and cobwebs, then I'd lean against his window and look out across the recreation ground. The view from his room was better than mine and it didn't upset me at all. I didn't do it often, only sometimes. And sometimes, when I leant against the window, I almost imagined that I could see him out there. Not really, because I don't believe in that sort of thing, but just sometimes.

It used to happen in the evenings mainly, on warm sunny evenings as dusk fell. Just as sometimes I'd hear him again in the bedroom next to mine. I'd hear him breathing: imagine it, that is, because I don't believe in ghosts. In fact, that sort of talk makes me mad. I want to scream when I hear people talking about auras and getting in contact with other worlds. It's rubbish, but I never say that. I'm someone who's supposed to have an opinion about death, but I'm always the one who keeps quiet.

'I don't know *what* you're talking about, Juliet!' Gran stares stiffly at Mum. 'I didn't say anything special.'

Dad gets up. He can't deal with this.

'You *do* know,' Mum's voice is low, as if she's speaking

from the depths. 'I don't want you to talk like that, not any more, Anna. I've come here, *we've* come here to make a new start. And that's what we're going to do.'

Dad coughs. He's sidling towards the back door. Mum forces herself to go on.

'And if you don't want to do that, Anna, maybe you need to think about living somewhere –' But Mum doesn't finish her sentence. Can't, probably, because the fact is Gran has sold her house and moved in with us. She doesn't have anywhere else to go. We all know it.

'So please, Anna, don't talk like that any more!' Mum's voice is swamped in unshed tears. She stares out over the wide, wordless sea. Sometimes I feel as though her silences will smother me.

And I'm waiting, with my breath held in, waiting for something else to happen. Because, whatever Mum says, Gran is still right about one thing: whenever there is a day of perfect summer sun, I remember Tom and I sometimes look up and almost expect to see him there.

My back and stomach are moist and there is no breath of air anywhere. I close my eyes and blink because the sea is too bright.

'Well, Juliet, I'm very sorry,' says Gran. 'I am sad and I am sorry that you feel like that. I only wanted to say –' She doesn't finish her sentence either. There's no point. She won't ever leave us now and anyway Mum has already rushed indoors.

Dad returns, polishing his glasses with his handkerchief. He smiles at the view and he nods to himself. Then he pops his glasses back on.

'Pizza?' he asks nervously. 'Or maybe a takeaway? I saw a couple of places in town.' He's glancing at Luke and me. 'How about it? We could walk along the cliff path.'

4

Luke looks at me. I nod. Dad smiles.

'Mother?' he turns to Gran. 'Do you fancy a walk? A spot of air?'

'No. I don't fancy a walk. You think there is *air* for walking in this heat? You must be mad.'

'Helen?'

'Yes. Sure, but –'

'OK, Helen. Maybe you're right. Maybe you'd better stay. Just for now.' His eyes stray towards the house. 'So is that all right with everyone?'

'Of course it's all right,' Gran smiles. She comes over to stroke my hair. 'Of course Helen doesn't mind staying behind with her foolish old grandmother. It's better than shaking her stomach around all over the streets. And in such heat.' Then she says what she always says, 'Such lovely hair! Such lovely hair my Helen has.' She smoothes it back from my forehead. I tilt my face up so that she can kiss me and when she does, I smell chocolate on her old, velvet skin.

'Your mother,' she whispers as Dad closes the garden gate, 'your poor mother.'

'I know.' My cheek is touching the silky stuff of her blouse. 'I know.'

'My sister,' Gran continues, 'my little sister, Edith –'

'I know.'

'She had such hair. Such beautiful, golden hair! But me? I get the chicken's hair in the family. Just my luck, eh?' She pats hers, which still sticks up in thick, white tufts.

I smile into her bosom which is hidden behind its layer of vest and petticoat, even on a day like this. It isn't only chicken's hair that Gran has. It's chicken's everything, with her scaly legs, round, darting eyes and the endless cluck, cluck of her tongue.

'But you, Helen,' as she lifts my hair from the nape of my

neck I feel a breath of cool air, 'but you, Helen, you have the beautiful hair my little Edith had. But she looked after it. She sat at the dressing table in our room and every night she's brushing it, again and again.' Gran's stroking mine, trying to drag her fingers through it. 'She brushes it every morning and every night so that it shines like gold. And you, Helen, this is what you should do. If only your mother had taught you.'

'She did, Gran, she really tried.' I'm not that much of a traitor.

'I know. I know your poor mother has tried. And I know how hard it has been for her.'

But Gran doesn't and I don't think she ever will. And sometimes I think that if I was only braver, I'd run to the nearest hairdresser and say 'cut it off, cut it all off'. And there it would be on the floor, every precious golden curl of the Kopperberg family hair. I'd have it shaved, if I dared. But I'm not brave like that. Not now.

I just sit quiet and let my grandmother rake back my hair. Her rings catch, then snag, and as I turn my head from side to side, trying to get free, something catches my eye.

A boat is sailing slowly past. I can hear the throb of its engines. A man's voice drifts up on the hot, thick air. I watch as it moves through the water.

'My goodness,' Gran has followed my gaze. 'Do you see *that*, Helen? A *green* boat! How unusual that is!'

'Why?'

'It's unlucky, of course. Anyone will tell you that. Why, when I was a young woman growing up here, nobody, no proper sailor would ever have gone to sea in a *green* boat. *So* unlucky it is!'

'Why?'

'Why? There's no "why". It's just the way it is. Though some people said that it was stealing the colour from the

6

sea. But it's tradition, Helen, that's what it is.'

'What about the pilot boats? They're green.'

'Yes. I know. What can one do? It's the same every-where. There are no standards now. Not like when we were young. People just don't care about the traditions. That is why they have green pilot boats.'

I open my mouth to speak, but don't. What's the point? Down there, on the green boat, something is running to and fro. A dog is barking. It's scaring off the seagulls which whirl and turn in the green boat's wake. I pick up Dad's binocu-lars. One of the men wears a red sweater, and shorts. He's at the side of the boat and I can see his bare, brown legs. He looks exactly like a pirate. I watch him lean out and pick up one of the moorings just off the Point.

I open my mouth then shut it again: there's nobody to talk to here. There's no one to nudge and say, 'Hey, do you think those are *pirates* down there?' My family would take a look and smile at me. 'No, Helen,' they'd reply, 'those aren't pirates. This is South Wales, not the South China Seas.'

But my friend Pat would have understood. She'd have trained the binoculars on those blokes and she'd have said, 'Yum, yum!'

As we sit down to supper Dad remarks that they saw brambles on their way back from the takeaway; the berries are ripening nicely. Gran agrees, Pembrokeshire is famous for its blackberries. They'd all lived on them in the long, sunny autumns, after the war, when food was so scarce. Blackberries and mushrooms, those are the fruits of autumn, just as they had been in her home country of Hol-land. There, they'd had a cellar full of jams and pickles, and lost the lot when the Nazis invaded. Such a waste. Such a terrible waste. Gran shakes her head but smiles at Mum, who nods. She has autumn memories too: Mum may have

7

grown up in suburbia a generation later, and *her* mother may have made blackberry and apple purée and put it in the freezer, but it's something. She had also picked blackberries, and mushrooms, on the commons and in the Surrey hills. At least they agreed about that.

'Shall *we* go blackberrying, Mum?' I ask as we wash up. 'We could go along the cliff path tomorrow. Term's only just started so there isn't much homework, and as I don't know anyone here, there's not a lot to do . . . We can go after school.'

'Why not?' Mum stares past me and out to sea, but her tone is pleasant. She even smiles. '*You* go, Helen. I won't bother.' She turns towards me. She isn't upset. She just looks bored. 'You go and pick blackberries, if that's what you want to do. You can take your grandmother, and Luke, but don't ask me to help. I've done that and I'm sick of it. I want to do something else.'

'Right.' I feel so stupid.

Does she honestly think that I'm dying to spend a couple of hours blackberrying with a kid and an old age pensioner? I only said it because her silences get me down and I thought it might cheer her up. The truth is she hasn't thought about me at all. She's somewhere else altogether, with him, not me. Now she dries her hands briskly and smiles.

'Do you know, Helen, I think I'm going to like it here. I think it's going to be all right. Don't you?'

'Yes.'

'And what's more,' her voice is confident and cheerful, 'I think he'd be glad that we've come. He was always so happy here. I think it's what he would have wanted. Don't you?'

What can I say? She puts her arm around me. I listen as she tells me about him: how he'd loved our seaside holidays; how perfect everything had always been. And it was. She's right about that. We were happy. The trouble is, I don't think she ever remembers that I was there. Still, I know things about Tom that she doesn't even imagine, secret things that he shared only with me. One day I might tell her, but not yet, because it is a secret. And I promised him that I would never ever tell.

Chapter 2

I've never told anyone about the Red Rock Dive, except Pat
and that was years later, so it didn't count. It happened at
the weekend, on a Saturday, I think, and at the end of our
holiday. Mum and Dad were out so Gran was in charge of
us, or me at least. She'd cooked lunch, a Dutch speciality,
and I hadn't liked it. I can remember sitting there and messing with it because I hated the shiny red colour. It was
something with beetroot, and I'd made scummy red stains
on the clean, embroidered cloth. Gran sighed and grumbled that I, a great big girl who'd been in school for ages,
still couldn't eat up nicely. She grumbled that I hadn't been
brought up properly and so didn't have any decent man-
ners. She didn't mention it that time but I knew that she was
thinking about her little sister, Edith, who had always done
everything very nicely indeed. Edith had had a proper
Dutch upbringing and would have eaten up her beetroot
and then asked for more. Well, Gran continued, perhaps it
was time I did the same! She told me that I'd have to sit
there until I'd finished up the whole plateful of food. She
looked at her watch and said that she didn't care if it took all
day. I was amazed. I can remember glancing at Tom for
help. I've always been a slow eater. When I couldn't swal-
low stuff, Mum let me spit it out in the loo. There didn't
seem much chance of that now, with Gran sitting there like
a witch.

'Eat it,' Tom said. 'Eat it up, Helen, and I'll give you a
wish. Anything you like.'

'What? Anything?' I said, through the first mouthful. 'Like a real pony of my very own?'

'Well, it has to be something that I can give, or do, doesn't it?'

'Like playing Monopoly, non-stop, all day?'

'Ye-es.' I knew from his tone that he didn't think much of that idea either.

'I know,' I said. 'I know *exactly* what I want, and you'll like it, Tom, you'll love it. So it's a wish for you as well.' I was so proud of myself.

'Can't be Monopoly,' he grinned, 'that's a relief. Now eat up. Please?'

I did. I even ate the bits off the tablecloth.

'So, Helen,' said Gran, coming back in, 'you can behave properly, if you try.'

She was right, in her way, but I didn't understand her at all when I was little. I thought she was a witch and a foreign witch too and I was scared of her. I didn't know about the war and the horrible things that had happened to her and her family when the Nazis invaded Holland. I just knew that I made her wild. Tom didn't, but for some reason that was never clear, I did. Sometimes I suspected that she didn't like me at all.

'Well,' Tom grinned as Gran took my emptied plate into the kitchen, 'what's it to be?'

'The Red Rock Dive,' I whispered back. I was breathless with the excitement of thinking of something so clever, so unexpected.

'But –' Tom frowned. Then I remembered: it was forbidden. We were not allowed to do that ever.

The Red Rock Dive was notorious around here. It was a thing boys did to prove themselves and younger children always talked about, under their breath. Even if other boys, other local lads did it, or boasted about having done it, the Red Rock Dive was clearly forbidden to us. Now I realize that our parents put it like that to be tactful. There was never any question of my doing it. I couldn't have even climbed up the Red Rock. No, this was about boys and the things boys did. This was about Tom. He was forbidden to take the risk. And he had promised. They told us stories about a friend of Dad's who had done the dive in his youth and nearly killed himself. That was why they made Tom promise so early. They only made me promise too, as an afterthought, which was maybe why I forgot.

'Did you cross your fingers behind your back when you promised?' I whispered to Tom across the table.

'What?' He had stared at me, bewildered.

'Well,' I explained proudly, 'if you cross your fingers, like that, it means that the promise doesn't count. We do it all the time in school. When the teacher asks, "Do you promise to be quiet?" we say, "Yes, Miss", but secretly we all cross our fingers. Then we can be noisy without breaking our promise. Only Chloe doesn't, but she's a goody goody.' I was so pleased with myself for thinking of a way out.

Tom had grinned and I thought he was admiring me. Now, I think he was trying to stop himself from bursting out laughing at how stupid his little kid sister was. Secretly, and despite the crossed fingers, I was still worried: I didn't want him to break his promise, because that wasn't like him at all, and I didn't want him to take the risk.

'I could have another wish, couldn't I, Tom?' I asked. 'It'd still work, wouldn't it, with a different wish? I could take *that* wish back and have another . . . if you like, Tom?'

He didn't reply.

'You can do that with wishes, can't you?' Somewhere in the back of my mind, I had begun to be afraid. Now, I

12

didn't want him to do the Red Rock Dive. It had always looked too high.

'It's OK,' he muttered as we finished our fruit, 'it's OK, Helen. If that's your wish, I'll do it. I promised I would.' He got up from the table and smiled at me but I couldn't smile back. I remembered the way the water raced through the pool at the base of the Red Rock and how the sun glinted on the wet, red edges below.

'You could do my wish later, couldn't you, Tom? It doesn't have to be today. You could do it next year or in a hundred years. Couldn't you? Tom?' I tried again.

'No! I couldn't! If I'm going to do it, Helen, it's got to be today.' His voice was unexpectedly loud.

I thought that he was angry with me. Now I think that he was angry with himself. He was afraid of the dive, even more afraid of it than I was. That was what made him angry. I followed him round as he got his towel and his trunks. I listened in astonishment as he lied to Gran. He said that he was taking me to catch crabs.

'Good,' Gran said. 'What a lucky little girl you are to have such a kind brother.' She waved us goodbye and never suspected a thing. She trusted Tom, even if she didn't trust me.

We passed the landing stage where other children were crouching down with buckets and sticks, catching crabs, but we didn't stop. Tom quickened his pace. I needed to run to keep up. It wasn't like him to walk too fast, but it wasn't like him to break his word, either, so I ran after him with my breath coming in gusts and starts.

That afternoon our beach wasn't deserted and I was annoyed. I always thought other people were trespassing. In my family, we referred to it as 'our beach' and I thought that in some way it did belong to us. Now I realize that it was usually deserted because it was far away. It couldn't be reached by car and the walk across the cliffs took half an hour and was followed by the treacherous slope down. That afternoon I scowled at some children I spotted down there, playing at the water's edge. A couple of older boys were squatting on the rocks slinging pebbles at cans. I thought I recognized one of the girls. She lived in cottages near Gran but I didn't know her name. She was playing by herself but she looked up as we approached, and she flipped a mat of black hair away from her face.

'Hey,' I blurted out. 'You'll never guess what my brother is going to do!'

'What, then?' Her expression was guarded.

'He's going to dive off the Red Rock!' I had suddenly realized that the presence of children made the whole thing more exciting still.

'And?' She stared at Tom, then glanced indifferently at me.

I shrugged and scampered after Tom, tongue-tied, but when I looked back the girl was watching us. She was shielding her eyes and I knew why. She was squinting at the very top of the Red Rock, and she was impressed. When I turned round again the kids had left off digging. They were all following us and I was excited and so proud.

I stared as Tom stripped off and I remember his clean, sunburnt toes curled over the rocks as he stepped up. He put his foot on a ledge, pressed his body close to the rock and began to climb. I wasn't afraid now. Oh no. I was happy and wild with joy. A skinny little boy, who was even smaller than me, stood close to my elbow. His bare stick of a shoulder touched mine.

'Can I watch?' he asked. He was shivering and his nose was bunged up with snot.

'Yes. If you like,' I was delighted that he had asked my permission. 'But you have to pay.'

14

I don't know why I said it because I didn't want his money. I suppose I thought it would make this great event even more important. The little boy didn't object. He turned away and began to feel in the pockets of his shorts.

'I've only got this,' he clutched a packet of matches, rattled it sadly, then held it out. I took it and told him that matches were fine. I was bored with him and I only wanted to watch Tom. I squatted down and looked up, scowling against the sun. Tom was almost at the top. The older boys were coming over now, and the girl too.

'He's *my* brother!' I reminded everyone, jumping up and pointing as though they couldn't see. 'He's my brother, Tom.'

Now he was standing above the drop. I looked down into the pool at the base of the rocks where he must dive, and it was too small. My glance lingered over the rough, red edges, which the sea had sharpened into claws. I blinked and looked away towards the horizon which was soft and blue. When I looked back, he was still standing on the edge, staring down.

Sometimes I can see him still.

'He's not going to do it,' one of the children said.

'He *is*!' I screamed. 'He's *my* brother and he *is* going to do it!'

'Well he shouldn't, that's all I can say. Not with the tide on the turn. He'd be a fool to try now.' The boy who spoke was a fair-haired lad of Tom's age, or maybe older. He had the local accent that Gran was so worried we might copy. He was deeply sunburnt and somehow he looked as though he might know about tides and things to do with the sea.

'Tell him not to,' he said to me, but I looked away and fiddled with a shell. I didn't want to hear .

'Don't!' He yelled, cupping his hands, but the waves and the breeze scattered the sound.

15

Suddenly and helplessly, I regretted ever having made that wish. I watched another wave roll in over the pool and I felt sick. I watched a lazy trail of seaweed rise and fall and I watched the sea draw back like lips from old, bared teeth. Tom didn't move. I wanted to call up too. I wanted to beg him to stop.

'He doesn't *dare*.' The thin girl, who had been standing at the back, turned to leave.

'He *does*,' I shrieked, 'you've got to wait. You mustn't go!'

'Tourists: they haven't got the guts,' another older boy turned away.

'Don't!' I was desperate to make them stop. 'He'll do it! He *will*.'

'He's a coward,' muttered the girl under her breath.

'He *isn't*. He's . . .' I held out my arms. I couldn't let them go. The girl gave me a push. I shoved her back, and slipped. I grabbed at the air, slipped further and fell into the pool. Another wave flung me back against the rocks. Weed touched my face and mouth. I saw their outstretched hands but couldn't reach. I couldn't thrust the water from me as the turning tide dragged me under and I didn't even try.

Then he dived. Somehow, in that second Tom dived and got it right so that he came up between me and the rocks. The children rushed back and dragged me on to the rocks where I was massively sick into a pool. When they were satisfied that I wasn't dead, they left me and clustered around Tom. Only the little boy stayed by me. He bent over, his body touching mine. I thought he was examining the lumps of beetroot, which I had vomited up.

'Have you still got them?' he asked.

'Got what?' I was wiping sick from my mouth.

'My matches,' he said. We looked into the water and I thought I saw them for a moment before another wave

16

swept them from view. His mouth puckered and I thought he was going to cry because he was sorry for me and because he was glad that I hadn't drowned.

'I'm all right,' I said bravely, but he wasn't interested in me. He had already moved away. None of the children were concerned with me. They were all crowding round Tom. I pushed my way through and then I saw what had happened. The rocks had cut him from shoulder to waist. His whole back was red with blood. I looked and was sick again and again.

'Helen,' he said, 'you're not to tell.'

I shook my head, too sick to speak, but I understood exactly what he meant.

The older boy, the sunburnt one looked carefully at Tom's injuries. He said that they weren't that deep so he'd be all right. It was a mess but the cuts would heal. Then he took off his own T-shirt and handed it to Tom. We all understood why: it was to cover up that bloody mess. Tom nodded and eased the garment over his head. We all watched in silence and knew that we would never tell. The other children continued staring as we got to our feet, walked across the beach and began the climb back to the top.

Halfway up the cliff path I stopped, and Tom bumped into me.

'I lost them,' I said suddenly, remembering the matches. I felt tears beginning to trickle down my cheeks. 'I dropped my little box of matches when I fell in.' I tried to turn round on the steep slope, and go back, but he was in my way. 'They'll be spoilt, won't they and lost at the very bottom of the sea?' It felt like tragedy and suddenly I began to cry.

'Do you want me to dive in again?' he asked. I looked into his face, which was almost touching mine, and I saw something I'd never seen before: Tom was crying too. I

17

didn't say anything. I just shook my head and shut up and scrambled back up the slippery path to the top of the cliff. From there I looked down: all the children had returned to the water's edge except one, who was watching us as we walked away.

At home, Tom lied again. He kept his back hidden as long as he could, then he said he'd fallen off his bike. When Mum and Dad asked me, I shrugged and pulled a face.

Later that summer, when it was safe, Tom and I sometimes let our eyes meet, but we didn't talk about the Red Rock Dive again. I've never told anyone except Pat and that doesn't really count because by then Tom was dead. It's just that sometimes, when Mum is going on and on, I remember it. It's the one thing she'll never know about Tom.

Chapter 3

'Helen? Is Helen Kopperberg here?' Next day in school, Mrs Cable is trying to read my name from the scrap of paper she has brought into the classroom. She's a small, pink-cheeked teacher and she's interrupted a maths lesson, which pleases most of my group. They're glancing up and beginning to chat. I keep my head down as she stumbles over my name again. I quite like maths. I'm wondering if I can get away with not identifying myself. I've guessed what it's about and I don't want to know. Back home in my other school this sort of thing kept happening. I was always being called out of class, but I'd hoped it would be different here.

No one knows me, or us, in this town so I'd hoped for a change. I could be wrong, of course. This time it could be nothing more than a helpful member of staff informing me that the sports bag I lost on the second day of term has been found, and that yes, my new trainers are still in it. But some-how I don't think so.

It never is anything ordinary like that. Half the class has already turned round and identified me, so there's no escape. It's some girl. 'This poor year ten student,' Mrs Cable breathlessly informs me as we step outside into the corridor.

'Nobody can do a thing with her. She's in floods of tears, poor thing. It's her father, you see. He . . . died, we think, just this last week.' She pauses and looks at me. She's hoping that I'll make it easy for her, that I'll offer to help. But I don't. She'll have to spell it out.

'So, Helena, and what a pretty name, if you don't mind me saying so, foreign, is it?'

'It's not Helena. It's Helen.'

'Oh well, near enough! Now Helena, I hope you don't mind, dear, but of course everyone here knows about "Life Long" and the wonderful work your parents do in this field. So, we just wondered if you could possibly help out. It's a very special case. They're a local family, and . . .'

This is the moment to refuse.

'If you could just have a word with poor Samantha. She is so upset. But you mustn't feel obliged, Helena.'

Not obliged! With her standing there, all flushed and wringing her hands? Does she really think it's possible for me to say 'no' and walk back into class?

If only.

But why not? Why does it feel so hard to say 'no'? Even as I'm thinking about it, I can feel my chance of escape ebbing away. I should have spoken out instantly. 'Sorry,' I should have said, 'but this isn't anything to do with me. I'm only a pupil here and I don't want to get involved.' That would have finished it. She might have marked me down as a selfish bitch, but so what? She wouldn't have asked me again.

'It'll only take a few minutes, Helena.' Her tone is less friendly.

I want to laugh, to tell her that she's wrong. Hopelessly, uselessly, endlessly wrong. A few minutes! We've done seven years' hard labour in my family and nothing is right yet.

'There we are.' She opens a door off the corridor into a hot, white room. I didn't even know it was here.

There are two white beds on either side and an old-fashioned white sink in the middle. A girl is bending over, splashing water on her face. We've startled her and she's annoyed. I see it at once, as she swings round to face us. Her eyes are swollen, her nose and lips puffed out. Mascara has run and streaked. The look on her face is one of sheer, unadulterated hate.

Does Mrs Cable recognize it? Is that why she's backing out so hastily? She finishes her drivel about 'the two of us having so much in common' then she closes the door behind me. I feel as if I've been shut in with something that has been cornered and caged.

'I'm Helen,' I say, because I've got to say something.

'There's no point,' she replies, 'you needn't waste your time.' She drags her black hair across her face like a limp, wet wing. 'There's no point in your coming in here to make nice conversation with me because I don't want to be nice. I don't even want to talk. And we've nothing in common. You might as well clear off. You can't trick me into being sensible, because I won't. Not any longer.'

She's right of course. It's what people always try and do. They keep on and on at you until in the end you say, 'Yes, I'm fine, I'm absolutely brilliant. Even though my brother has just died, life's never been better!' Then they feel comfortable. They don't have to worry about poor old you anymore and they can go on their way.

I'm being unfair, but I don't care. I've had enough of being sensible too, and I don't want to be here either. Overhead, up near the white ceiling, an electric bar fire is blazing red. No wonder the room is stifling. The white cupboard in the corner has a red cross painted on the door. There's a pile of dusty leaflets in a box: *Sex and YOU!* and *Marriage and YOU!* But they haven't got one for this. There's no *Death and YOU!*

This girl, Samantha, turns her back on me. She takes a make-up purse from her school bag, mops up the black streaks on her cheeks, then unfurls the little brush and loads more mascara on. She slaps creme powder on to her red nose, dabs blusher here and there and swallows hard before she turns to me.

'You think I'm crying because he's dead, don't you?' She has a rough, smoker's voice. 'Well, you're wrong. You're all wrong. I'm glad he's dead and I wish I'd done it myself. I'm only crying because –' She bites her lip. I look in the mirror and I see her new face dissolve. I don't try to stop her crying. I just leave her to it.

I don't go back to maths. I find the toilets, lock the door and then lean back. It's always the same, isn't it? Pee and warm crap and the cold smoke left by the last one to snatch a fag. Then there's that stuff they always use on the floors: pine, but muddied and sour. I'm not a smoker so I just sit there with my pants down and the tears streaming over my face.

The thing is, I've learnt the technique. I can cry without my face swelling up or letting out a single sound. And that's the one trick that people like my father never teach you in counselling even though it's the one thing that might help. When the bell rings I get up, wash my hands and go back into class. I forget instantly and to look at me, you'd never suspect a thing.

I don't think about Samantha either. I just forget her too. Until now, that is, when I'm walking home along the cliff path. It's longer than the road way, but nicer. It would make a good place to run, with lots of little hilly bits and a view. Pat would have called it ideal. But I haven't done any running since we moved here. I might have, if I hadn't lost my running shoes and if I wasn't alone. I could have sprinted along this stretch of the cliff path right above where the green pirate boat is still moored off the Point. If Pat was with me, we could have waved at the guys on board, or at least barked at the dog. Pat would have done that. She was always up for a laugh. She never cared what other people thought of her. You don't expect that from a vicar's daughter, do you? But that was Pat. And I miss her so.

I miss her dreadfully and I think that's why I've started thinking about Samantha. She reminds me of Pat. It's not physical, because Pat is sandy-haired and freckly and as thin as a lad. Not anorexic thin, or anything like that, just slim and muscular because she's a runner. Samantha is plump and dark and there's nothing of a lad about her. So, it's not looks. It's attitude. It's that 'I don't give a toss what you think about me' thing. That's what I think they share.

I envy them that, because I do care what people think. I care far too much. I hate to admit it but I suspect Mrs Cable was right when she said that Samantha and I had something in common. We do, but it's not because we've both lost 'a loved one' – God, how I hate that phrase! It makes me want to spit. No, it's not that. And I can't ever see Samantha putting on running shoes, but I *can* see her being interested in the pirate boat, and waving, if not whistling at the blokes. That's what we could share! She's the sort of girl Gran disapproves of, the sort of girl who would bark at that dog, even through tears. She's one of Gran's hussies and I envy her that. She said that awful thing about her father and though I don't believe her for a moment, I know how she feels. I wish I could say dreadful things like that, but I can't, and I don't think I ever will.

'He-len!' It's Luke's voice. 'He-len! Wait for me!'

I look back and forth along the empty cliff path but there's no one around. Then the undergrowth beside the cliff path begins to shake and Luke emerges looking twiggy and scratched. Leaves and bits of blackberry are caught on his new school sweatshirt, and he's a real mess.

'What were you doing in there?' I take his hand. It's hot

23

and rough with dirt and his face is red. He probably dropped something on the path, then lost it in the bushes and brambles as it rolled away. It'll be a ball, or marbles, or some really precious junk that he's only just found. Kids are like that, they make treasures out of dropped sticks, or someone else's rubbish, and when they lose them, they cry.

'What's up?'

'Nothing.' He shrugs several times, jerking his shoulders almost up to his ears. Maybe he's lost some more money. He's been doing that a lot recently. He isn't interested in it himself and I think he gives it away to other children. They get cross about it at home because he's always asking for more.

'Did you lose something?' I ask again.

'Not really.' He's looking at his feet.

'I can have a look for you. If you like.'

'It doesn't matter. It wasn't anything special.' He begins to walk away.

We're nearly home now. Luke should have been in half an hour ago because the primary school is nearer than my school and it comes out earlier so he must have been fooling about a lot. I don't think he's supposed to take the cliff path at all, especially not on his own. I won't say anything. It's been hard enough for Mum and Dad to let him out of their sight at all and I don't want to cause a stir. This is a pretty safe sort of place: an end of the line little town, and literally the last stop for the train. It has to go back the way it's come after this.

That's one of the reasons Mum and Dad decided to move down here. The coast may be dangerous and littered with wrecks but none of us plans on going to sea; and as I've said, they don't know about the Red Rock Dive, and I'm not going to tell them. So far as they're concerned, this is a safer place to bring us up: no clubs, no drugs and definitely fewer roads. So, who am I to rock the boat? Anyway, clubs and drugs aren't my thing, if I'm honest. I'd still be taller than most of the blokes in a club, whatever I'd popped.

'Do you know what I saw?' I shake Luke's hand gently. He seems quiet this afternoon and I want to cheer him up.

'No.'

'A pirate ship!'

'Oh.'

'It was just back there. It's that green boat anchored off the Point. You passed it, but I don't expect you knew what it was.'

'Oh. That . . .' He's scuffing his shoes along in the dust. 'That's not a pirate boat, Helen. That's the *Black Pig*. That's Mr Owens' boat.'

'Who's Mr Owens?'

'The man who drowned. Don't you know anything?' He pulls his hand from mine and runs on ahead.

I'm irritated. I shout at him to stop being such a prat. He's spoilt his sweater and his new school shoes. Gran will be cross when she sees the damage and I'll have to put it right. Doesn't he care?

'How do you know about Mr Owens, anyway?' I ask when I catch him up.

He shrugs again and won't say and even kicks up more dirt. I snatch hold of his hand and I grip it so tightly he can't get away.

At our gate I open it, push Luke inside and then I let him go. I glance back along the path, where the bushes and brambles have twitched and then settled down, as if some rush of heated summer air has just blown through. Then I look back at the unlucky boat on the flat, blue sea.

25

Chapter 4

Nobody believes me when I say that I like cleaning shoes, but I do. I like rubbing the oily colours into the leather; one minute it's dull and smudged, then, after a few brush strokes, it's shining again. It's not just as good as new, it's better because everyone likes having their shoes looking good. They're grateful, especially older people, like Gran. She forgives me loads of things when I polish her shoes. She even forgets how badly I've been brought up.

Pat got me into this shoe-cleaning obsession. Her father, the Reverend Rook or Rooky, as he was called, always said that you could get away with being shabby so long as your shoes were shiny. His were, although Pat's whole family took shabbiness to a new art form. If I'm truthful the Rook family made church mice look well-dressed. Pat used to joke that she was so used to getting all her clothes from jumble sales, that she might as well pick up her boyfriends there too. They couldn't have been any more trouble than the ones she got brand new so maybe she was right. Pat Rook picked up more useless guys than you could find snails under a stone. But at least her shoes shone. And so did her father's, too.

Rooky wasn't picked-up jumble sale rubbish. He was a nice guy, a lovely father, and a good man, if that doesn't sound too sad. And even if it does, it's still true. I don't go to church, in fact you couldn't even drag me in now, but Pat's dad never mentioned it. He never cared and some-times I wondered how keen he was himself. But like I say, his shoes were always up to scratch –or should that be without a scratch? So, I can blame this all on him.

I squeeze out a long, black slither of cream, as soft and shiny as a slug and I start to work it into Luke's shoes. It shouldn't take long; his feet aren't that big and I feel guilty about having been mean to him. I like this job and I like the smell of bitter almonds that lingers on. Luke's certainly made a mess of these shoes. It's worse than I thought and I'm surprised. He used to be careful. He must have been kicking loads of stuff before I met up with him. I suppose kids do, don't they, and I shouldn't have been so cross. I can remember kicking drinks cans along the road. I even liked the racket! I kicked apples too, great big cooking apples which dropped off a neighbour's tree. Pat and I would slam them along the pavement, until they finally went splat, and I never thought about the mess.

I've spread a newspaper out on the table and now something catches my eye:

Search for Skipper of *Black Pig* Called Off

Coastguards announced that the search for David Owens was called off late last night. David Owens, the well-known local fisherman and skipper of the Black Pig, was reported lost at sea on Wednesday in a tragic accident. It is feared that Mr Owens, a non-swimmer, could not have survived another night in the water. Police and coastguards stress that they are keeping an open mind. An extensive search of the area will be continued. Neighbours are comforting Mr Owens' two younger children, Samantha and Wilfred. An attempt is being made to contact Mrs Sylvia Owens, who is believed to be in the Cardiff area. Christian, Mr Owen's eldest son, is helping with the search.

I look at the date. It's only last week. Has someone stuffed the paper to the bottom of the pile on purpose? I take the brush and begin to work up a shine. One of the cuts in the leather is so deep, it looks as if Luke must have been kicking glass.

There's a photo, a black and white shot of this David Owens. He's a giant of a man. He's grinning broadly and one front tooth is missing. He seems to be leaning over a white wall and his spade-like hands are clamped around the shoulders of two children who are standing in front of it. It's an odd pose. One child has his head down, so I can't see who it is. The other stares back at me, through wild black hair blown half across her face. She's much younger here, but I'd know Samantha anywhere. I'd recognize her and that look of hate. It's as bold and bad as David Owens' own. Gran would describe it as a hussy's look, and I'm ashamed to admit that I agree. So, that explains why she's been crying in school. Even if she didn't like the guy much, she wouldn't have wanted that sort of end for him, would she? No way! Poor old Sam.

Samantha and Wilfred Owens. Then I recognize the boy too. He's the dopey one in my tutor group, the one everybody calls Wiffy. It fits, because he hasn't been in school recently. He used to sit in the very front, beside the radiator and dead opposite the teacher. That's always the place for students who are very good or very bad and there was no doubt which Wiffy was. He never did any work at all. He just sat. Hardly any of the teachers bothered with him, but kids did. He got teased a lot and actually that teasing had looked a bit like bullying. I'd noticed it in my first week, but you can't get involved, not when you're new. I had thought everybody called him Wiffy to be beastly and because he smelt. I hadn't realized that it was a nickname and that he was really a Wilfred. You don't get many of those where I come from. Poor old Wiffy Owens. No wonder he hasn't

28

been in school. I finish Luke's shoes, then I do Gran's. I read the article once more then hide it away at the bottom of the pile, which is what we usually do.

Next morning Gran frowns, as she approaches the breakfast table. 'Just look at that!' she sighs.

I look, but can't see anything odd about breakfast, so I look at her. She appears just the same except that her shoes have an extra shine. I smile as I anticipate her thanks, but none come.

'I expect it's Luke.' She sighs again, but less crossly. She has a soft spot for him.

'What is it Gran?'

'This! There!' She's pointing to a black mark on the clean white cloth. It's my black mark. I hadn't noticed. I thought I was being careful. Gran's rubbing the spot with her finger and sniffing it, and I'm fed up.

I picture breakfast at Pat's: her mum and dad, her big sisters in boxer shorts and T-shirts, their red hair undone, their faces crumpled by sleep. Around the edges of the family would be a spattering of boyfriends and people passing through and anyone else who had turned up at the vicarage wanting a bed for the night. I remember them squeezed around the kitchen table. They'd be eating bread and jam and dropping crumbs, and passing the milk in big, supermarket bottles. If they'd finished the bread and jam, they'd be eating curry or pasta, or whatever was left in the fridge from the night before. Pat's kitchen was a good place to be and I never felt uncomfortable there. I never felt bad if I licked honey from a knife or put a damp spoon in the sugar. And the sun always shone. It came in through the cracked kitchen window and lit up the pinky-orange geranium that had sat on the edge of the sink for as long as I'd known the Rooks. And Pat's family never made a mark on a cloth because they didn't use one: just newspaper, smoothed nice and flat! I thought it was so odd when I first visited and Mum was worried about what sort of family the Rooks were, but we needn't have been concerned. Pat and her sisters knew more about world events than most adults. When I have a home and children, I shall spread newspaper on my table and if anyone makes a mark, I won't nag. I'll tear that bit off and throw it away.

Mum looks up from her tea. She glances at Gran and then at me.

'It doesn't matter about the mark,' she says, as if she's fed up too.

'I know it doesn't *matter*, because I can wash it!' Gran sniffs her fingers again. 'It is the leather polish, no? That I can tell. And I know how to wash the leather polish out. But it's a *shame*, no?'

'It's a shame,' Mum repeats, 'but –'

'But what, Juliet?' Gran's tone is challenging. 'You don't *like* your breakfast table to look nice? If that is so, then *tell* me, Juliet. This is your house. And you must have your house as you like. I know that too. And I am an old woman, with an old woman's old ways. If you do not *like* the good cloth, we do not have the good cloth. You can have the plastic, they are quite pretty, no? It is as simple as that. Eh, Helen? What you say? You *like* a cloth, a good white cloth to start the day? Or plastic?'

I look at the breakfast table which she had laid the night before, and which I've spoilt. She's put flowers in a little vase in the centre and the proper butter knife beside the dish. It looks lovely and I shouldn't have cleaned the shoes on it. It was stupid, but I'm not going to admit that. I've had enough.

'I prefer newspaper,' I quip.

Gran purses her lips. She touches the stain on the cloth.

30

'That is because you can *have* a cloth, Helen. When I was a girl like you, we didn't even have a table.'

The trouble is, it's true. When she was my age, Gran and her little sister Edith were eating their breakfasts, if that's what you can call them, in a Nazi concentration camp. There's no arguing with that, but what can I do? Nothing, except shut up and take my piece of toast.

'Wow! Thanks, Helen.' It's Luke. He runs in smiling, beaming actually, at his toe caps. They are so shiny he can see the reflection of his face. Good old Luke. It's what he does best and he's been doing it all his life. He comes in at exactly the right moment, like an actor on cue. Luke's like Hermes, the messenger in Ancient Greek mythology who makes the world go round, and he's been doing it since his birth. Luckily.

And luckily, though no one ever mentions it, Luke must have been on the way, conceived – if we have to be technical – before Tom died. For years I thought he was a replacement brother. I liked him, although he wasn't a patch on Tom, and it had always seemed a bit unrealistic of Mum and Dad to think he could be. Later, when I'd done reproduction in school, I counted back and breathed a sigh of relief: Luke wasn't their shot at a clone. I suppose other people must have made those calculations at the time, though they never talked about it when I was around. I didn't even know Mum was pregnant when Tom was killed. Afterwards, when it was obvious that she was, I just thought, oh well, now they're getting another one! And some parents do, don't they? But it wasn't like that with Mum and Dad. Luke was already on his way and he popped out, so to speak, just in time.

People still say 'Thank god for that baby' and 'What would your poor mother have done without him?' She

31

always replies, 'Gone back to work!' I'm not sure if she means it, but it's what she always says, and it's part of the reason we've come here, so that Mum can work. But sometimes I still hope that she'll reach out and put her arms around me, when someone talks like that. I want to hear her protest, 'But at least I've got my Helen.' But she never does.

Luke doesn't realize all this. He's just Luke, isn't he and a kid? And this morning, after making the correct entrance, he's pleased with his shoes. Kids are great like that. They're pleased with things and they smile at you and they fill up the silences. Lots of parents complain about the hard work of bringing up children. They make a huge deal out of sleepless nights and the expense of trainers and the phone bill. They grumble because their little children get up too early, then they grumble because their teenagers get up too late. Personally I think it's grown-ups who are such hard work. Pat says that living in a family is like balancing on razor wire and I think she's right.

When I have kids, I shan't grumble. I shall stick notices up with things like '*Smiling not nagging*', and when I'm beastly to them, I shall say I'm sorry. Then I'll smile at them over the newspaper, and try not to do it again.

'Would you polish my shoes?' Mum asks suddenly.

'Sure. Do you want them now?'

'No, no. This evening will be fine. It's for my interview tomorrow.'

'What interview?' Dad is put out. 'What interview, Juliet? It's the first I've heard of it.' Gran keeps her eyes down and butters a small piece of toast.

'It's only at the garden centre, Charles.'

'The garden centre! Juliet?'

Mum's grinning. She was an architect before. Her eyes are sparkling as she challenges Dad but I think it's definitely time for school. I haven't had a bite of my toast but this is something they can do all by themselves.

'Come on,' I say to Luke, and I give him a shove.

Outside the house he turns in the wrong direction. It's a good job I'm with him. Even though we're in time now, he'd be late if he went by the cliff path.

I take his hand. I can remember day-dreaming and going the wrong way and not caring, either. Tom used to take my hand then. He used to keep me on track.

He thought I was cute and he liked taking me around. The summer that he got his new bike, when he was eleven or twelve, and had started at the comprehensive, he made the bike-cart. He used old pram wheels, with a seat in the middle for me and it hitched on the back of his bike. Mum and Dad were worried at first and insisted that we wore helmets. We did, even though they were uncomfortable and hot, and even though nobody else did. But nobody laughed either, because of Tom. He was like that. Soon all the kids in the neighbourhood were wearing helmets. He'd started the trend. He even took me to school in the bike-cart. He'd let other kids have a go, a quick whiz round the playground, if they held on properly. My friends used to groan that it wasn't fair, their big brothers never did anything nice like that. But Tom was special: everybody recognized that.

'Helen?' Luke stops. He's staring down at his shoes.

'What?'

'Couldn't we go the other way?' He looks up at the bright sky.

'Not really.'

He bites his lip.

'What's wrong with this way?' I ask. He wriggles about, like a baby bird flexing its wings. I shift my rucksack so that I can hold his hand more comfortably, then I set off again with him in tow. Ahead of us, a small group of people is standing on the pavement beside a whitewashed wall. I hurry Luke past, but he looks back.

'Come on,' I tug his hand. I'm sick of him dawdling. Then I recognize the wall. This is where that man was standing, the giant of a man who was leaning over and who had now drowned. One of these terraced houses must be his.

'Hiyah!' It's Wiffy. Samantha is there too, but she doesn't acknowledge me. Only a middle-aged woman in a nightie, with her feet in old pink slippers and long hair trailing down her back smiles. Is she Sylvia, the mother people were trying to locate in Cardiff? I smile back uncertainly. I should stop and say 'hello' to Wiffy, at least, if not to Sam. After all, he's in my tutor group and I know how it feels when people walk past.

'Hiyah!' Wiffy says again and bounds over.

Now Luke wants to drag me off but Wiffy is in the way. He's looking at me intently and I can see the breakfast cereal stuck between his teeth.

'I saw you yesterday,' he says, 'and the day before. But you didn't see me.' There's sleep in the corners of his eyes, where he hasn't washed and I step back. I don't know what to say to him but it doesn't matter. Wiffy doesn't mind.

'Have you seen the flame?' he asks, cheerfully.

'What flame?' I look around stupidly, in case one of us is about to go up in a puff of smoke. He's pointing over my head.

'*That* flame!' He's grinning even more. 'Haven't you noticed it yet?'

'Noticed what?'

'The flame! You must have. You've got the best view.'

'Shut up!' Samantha snaps. 'Shut up about your stupid flame, you're doing my head in!'

Her make-up is perfect now, her cigarette is inserted between carefully painted purple lips. She takes a drag then

34

holds a packet out to me. I shake my head.

'Lucky you,' she says chattily, 'but I have to, for my nerves. I'm giving it up soon. But not yet.' She takes another thirsty drag.

'He yours?' She nods at Luke.

'Yes.' I'm not quite sure what she means.

She laughs, then slaps Wiffy on the back.

'And he's mine! What d'you think of that? Some brother, eh?'

Wiffy suddenly runs at her as though he'll knock her down but she only laughs at him and before I can say anything, Luke rips his hand free from mine. He tears up the pavement in his new, shiny shoes, and he doesn't stop. He carries on and runs straight in front of a small red van and I hear the squeal of brakes.

Chapter 5

'You OK?' Someone is speaking to me through smoke. I can't feel the heat or hear the crackle, but it's smoke, all the same. It's an acrid smell and strong and it reminds me of how Dad smells when he's been to a pub.

'Where's Luke?' I rub my hands over my face. I need to clear my head.

'Luke!' I shout, when no one answers.

Above me, against a bright blue sky, the group of people are shaking their heads. They look at each other, then down at me.

'Luke? Who's Luke?' They're twittering amongst themselves like birds perched close on a branch, but they don't speak to me.

'Luke!' I'm trying to speak clearly through fluttering lips. I'm trying to find my feet too. 'Luke! Where's Luke?'

'It's her *brother*,' mouths Samantha.

'Oh. Does she mean that little boy?' another asks, as though I'm not there.

'That's right. That's *Luke*. Where is he?' I beg. 'Is he all right?' I want to get up.

A tall man who has been standing at the back of the group squats down beside me.

'It's OK,' he says. 'Your little brother is fine. I just saw him run through the school gate. Don't worry. He didn't see what happened to you. He didn't see you faint.'

I can't say anything. He pulls down the edge of my skirt that has been hitched up and he brushes something from it.

I look at him, and at them, and I can't begin to explain. I cannot put into words what I thought I saw out there in the road because they couldn't possibly understand.

The man holds out his hand and I put mine in his. Cool, rough-skinned fingers close over as he pulls me to my feet. He steadies my arm for a moment until the road and the white wall have stopped sliding, then he releases me. His eyes are grey, as blue-grey as the sea. I look down and see the thick, sun-bleached hairs on his legs. His toes are tanned and straight in open sandals. I'm staring and I know I'm beginning to blush. I feel such a fool. I can't believe I've actually fainted. I never do things like that.

'I'm sorry,' I mutter. 'I am so sorry.'

There's still stuff on my navy school skirt, leaves and a bit of sycamore, and I knock it off. Then, as I bend down to pick up my rucksack, I notice that my tights are sticking and pulling my skin. There are two big, bloodied holes on my knees and they're a mess. There is enough time to go back home but I don't want to. They'll make such a fuss.

'Did you miss your breakfast, then?' The woman in the nightie is leaning against the wall. She's holding some bushes aside to get a better look at me. Her black hair is caught on the broken off ends of branches and I can see where the white roots are growing out. She looks as though she hasn't slept for days, but her voice is soft.

'That must be it, mustn't it?' I nod and work up a smile. 'That's what my Gran always says: you mustn't miss breakfast, it's the most important meal of the day. It looks as though she's right.' She's staring at me as if I'm talking too much.

'Is that what your Gran says?' she repeats oddly.

'Yes, but I've never fainted before. Ever.'

'*I* have,' says Wiffy. 'I've fainted before. I've fainted millions of times!'

'You haven't,' snarls Sam.

'I *have*. I've even fainted twice. Once after the other. When –'

'Put a sock in it, Wiff!' The man's voice is sharp.

Wiffy Owens shuts up instantly. He closes his mouth and grins up at the tall guy. One of Wiffy's large brown eyes slides around in his face. The tall man touches Wiffy, gives his shoulder a sort of shake and suddenly I think I know who he is: he's 'the pirate' from the unlucky green boat. His was the voice I'd heard, floating up.

'Well, come on then, if you're coming,' Sam has finished her fag and tossed it to one side. '*I* could take *you* to the white room,' she offers, 'if you want.' She doesn't look at me but she laughs briefly.

'No! *I* can take her. Let *me*. Helen's in *my* class, so I must take her.' Wiffy is leaping around, trying to push his way between us like some daft puppy.

'*You* can't take her, you idiot.' Sam's tone is withering. 'She's a *girl*, in case you hadn't noticed.'

Wiffy's jaw drops. His full, red lips open and he sticks his tongue out to lick them round and round. Then he tilts his head too far back so that it looks as if he might topple over. He's staring up at the sky and sniffing the air like a dog. There's no doubt, Wiffy Owens is a bit odd. He lets his head loll even further and roll from side to side. He closes his eyes, furrows his brow and the edges of his nostrils quiver.

I can smell it too. Something *is* burning, and there is smoke. High above us and smeared across the autumn sky, a dark trail of smoke spreads like a stain.

'It's the refinery,' explains the man in the old red sweater, the man who must be Christian Owens. 'That's what you can smell. That's what that smoke is. It's always worse when the wind's in this direction.' He looks at me. 'If

38

you're not used to it, it can make you feel ill. I suppose it could even make you faint.'

'You coming or not?' Sam asks sharply. I nod. We walk up the road towards the school side by side, and in complete silence. Wiffy trails behind. I don't look back at Christian, but I'm sure that he and his mother stood and watched us until we were out of sight.

'Dear me, Helena,' Mrs Cable throws up her thin, pink hands when we enter the white room. 'Dear, dear! What a frightful mess. You have been in the wars, haven't you?' She flashes me a small, conspiratorial look as she inspects the damage. 'Everything all right is it? At home, Helena?' She breathes the question, rather than asks, and tips yellow disinfectant on to a cotton wool pad. I don't answer, just grit my teeth and peel down my tights. 'Now dear, be brave. This is going to sting a teeny-weeny bit, but I'll be as gentle as I can.'

She is gentle but thorough too, and I'm surprised. I've made mincemeat of my skin. She's right, it was some battle and my poor defeated knees really hurt now. I bet I'll have scars. That's another disadvantage of being so big. If you do fall over, or anything, you go with such a crash. But it's true what I said before, I've never fainted in my whole life.

'I tripped,' I tell Mrs Cable. 'I must have tripped, I think, over the kerb.' She nods. 'It was stupid of me,' I continue. 'I wasn't looking where I was going.'

She nods as if she doesn't believe me and I can't think why I lied.

'Yuk!' Sam is leaning against the door watching. From the revolted expression on her face, you'd think Mrs Cable was doing a quick spot of cardiac surgery and that it was my heart that was opened up, meaty red and throbbing, and not just my knees.

39

'Sam, if you go to Miss Evans in Room 42 I'm sure she'll give you a needle and some black thread. Then we can darn these holes, can't we, Helena?' Mrs Cable picks up the remains of my tights.

'I could go,' says Sam, 'but I wouldn't bother. When something's spoilt like that, I just stick it in the bin.'

Mrs Cable stops poking around for bits of grit. I'm expecting some pious remark like 'waste not, want not'. That's the sort of thing Gran would say, but Mrs Cable doesn't. She looks at Samantha, and then at me, and goes back to work. She's had to use tweezers on one bit, to lift up a flap of skin. I guess that she's about Mum's age. Her hair is cut in a neat bob with a fringe. It's shiny and clean and as nice as a child's. I bet she brushes it every night.

'I won't put plasters on them, dear, because it wants air to heal properly. But I'll use lint. That'll give you a bit of protection. And once you've mended those tights it will hardly show.'

'It will,' Sam contradicts. 'It'll look a sight. Shouldn't she get new ones, Miss?'

Mrs Cable snips out another neat, white square of lint.

'I don't see why not, girls,' she says, firming the tape across my skin. 'Where do you want to go, Sam?'

Samantha Owens stares. She pulls the matt of black hair back across her face. I'm sure she didn't expect Mrs Cable to say that.

'How about that little shop on the corner? They sell everything.' Mrs Cable is fishing change out of a small, blue purse. She drops it into Sam's hand. 'Count it again, dear, and we'll settle up later. Just don't be too long.'

'Poor cow,' says Sam as soon as we're out of the school gates. 'It's because she hasn't got kids of her own.'

'What is?'

40

'The way she fusses, the way she's all over you like a rash. Some girls say she's a lezzie, but I'm not sure, not really. I just think she's a bit sad.'

We're walking right past Luke's primary school. The murmur of kid's voices floats in the air. Instantly, desperately I want to see him. I want to be on my own and I wish she wasn't there. Then I could go in. I'd pretend he'd forgotten his hanky or his money and I'd just march in. Any excuse would do. I only want to see that he's safe. That's all.

'You OK?' Sam has stopped.

'Yes. Why?'

'You've gone as white as a ghost. You going to faint again?'

I feel white but I shrug it off. We choose the tights, or Sam does. I can't. I'm too worked up to do anything at all. She spends the rest of Mrs Cable's money on crisps and makes me eat the lot.

'So who's Tom?' she asks suddenly, pulling her hair over her face.

I fold the crisp packet up, over and over, until it is very small.

'Is it some bloke you know? Or was it that bloke in the red van?'

'No.' I turn into the toilets and she follows.

'Because that's what you *said*. That's what you called out.'

'Did I?'

'Yes. Honestly. You shouted "Tom! Stop, Tom!" And then you fainted. Wham. But I couldn't see anyone. Not anyone else, that is. Just your little brother running up the street to school. But he's Luke, isn't he?'

I nod.

'So, who's this other bloke? This Tom? What's with him, to make you faint like that?'

'Nothing. Not really. I think I was hungry. That's all.'

41

She shoves her hair back and waits, and I know that she doesn't believe me.

'He just . . . died. That's what Tom did.'

'What a bastard.'

'It wasn't like that,' I say, but I'm lying again, because that's exactly how it was. He didn't have to go and die. 'And it was ages ago, anyway. Just an accident.'

'Aren't they all?' She's lit up another fag and is picking the bits of tobacco from the tip of her tongue. 'So who was he then, this Tom?'

'My brother.'

Our eyes meet. Hers are as large as Wiffy's but black, and hard.

'Tom?' Her voice is hard now. 'Not your *brother* Tom?'

'Yes.'

'Not *the* Tom? Not the one who did that dive, the Red Rock Dive, years and years ago, when we were kids. You don't mean *him*?'

'Yes. I do.' Suddenly I know who she is. She's that girl, the one who was playing alone at the water's edge. She's the lippy, skinny one who had been on our beach. She's the one who called Tom a coward and gave me a shove.

'Christ,' she says. 'I never knew that. What a mess. What a rotten, stinking mess.' She taps the cigarette into the basin and runs hot water on the ash. Her hands are shaking, and mine too.

I recognize them now: they were all there on the beach, Sam, and little Wiffy with his box of matches, and Christian too. He was the boy who had shouted up and told Tom not to dive. He was the only one of us who had had any sense then.

'So,' she whispers, not looking at me, 'so he's . . .' She's too shocked to speak. Her voice has gone and I wish I hadn't told her. I never get used to people being so upset about the death of someone they barely knew.

'Yes.' I'm quite matter of fact. 'He's dead. He really is, though it was seven years ago.'

I ease the tights up over my poor old knees. They hurt a lot now and I almost wish I'd gone home. I chuck the empty pack in the bin and look at myself in the mirror. Sam keeps her face turned away.

'I can't believe it,' she says, starting another fag, 'that he's dead too.'

I remember her father and I feel so bad. That's it. That's why she minds so much and I should have shut up.

I don't know what more to say to her, so I shrug and push open the chipped swing door. I make my way back to class. I sort myself out. I spend break copying up. I don't like getting behind. When I've finished I lean back and cautiously stretch my legs out. Over my knees, the torn skin cracks.

Outside it is sunny, but I can still see the smoke. There's a dark plume rising from one of the chimneys on the refinery. As I watch, the wind, or something, must be changing. The smoke begins to billow like a grey sail filling, then it sinks down. It settles over the tongue of flame as though it will consume it or be consumed itself.

Someone else in the class jumps up. They slam all the windows shut, but the sour smell of smoke has already spread.

Chapter 6

I've been thinking about going back to the beach. I suggested it to Mum and she was keen, then she changed her mind. She got that job at the garden centre and started last week. In the end Dad was pleased. He fussed around with the car on her first morning at work but in the afternoon she told him not to bother. It's only three miles away so she'll go by bike. It'll do her good, she says. Dad was relieved. Although he runs the charity from his office at home he needs the car to visit clients. He also likes to use it to go out. Sometimes I think he just drives around and doesn't go anywhere at all.

Gran sighed when she saw Mum in jeans and her new garden centre T-shirt, and shook her head. I have to admit it's not like working as an architect, which is what Mum did before, but it seems to be fun. Mum's talked about nothing else since she started there. I like that, so I'm all for the change.

I invited Gran to come to the beach, although I was sure she wouldn't accept.

'It is a kind thought and you can be a good girl, Helen, when you try.' Gran had stroked back my hair and tried to tease a bit into a curl. When I was little she often tied my hair in rags before I went to bed. I liked her fussing over me in the evening, but the next morning I hated those curls, which sprung from the rags as plump and shiny as a headful of greasy sausages. I'd soak my hairbrush in water and wet them out as soon as I could. Gran would sulk. She insisted that those golden curls had made me look like a princess. Tom always laughed.

He said they made me look like Violet Elizabeth, that girl in my '*Just William*' book. Dad always read it to me as a bed-time story and if Tom was around he'd sit on the end of my bed and listen as well. 'Violet Elizabeth,' he'd tease, sticking his fingers into the sausages, ruffling them up. Spoiling them, Gran always said. She'd raise her hand to give him a playful slap, but she never did. No one was ever cross with Tom.

'You go to the beach, Helen, but don't be late.' Gran patted my cheek as though she had given up on my hair.

Had she curled it up on that Saturday when Tom and I went to the beach? I can't remember that now, although I can remember the way the beetroot still tasted of soil and how hot it was as we hurried across the hillocky grass on top of the cliff. I remember the blistering sun on the back of my neck and the flies in the shade on the other side of the wall. They flew up when we disturbed them and I didn't like that. Tom was walking so quickly and I was running to keep up. The dust scratched and itched. I'd got a stitch and had to stop. I'd crouched down and rubbed my side and smelt the wild thyme and trodden mint in the grass.

Today it's also hot. Not as hot as that summer seven years ago, but hot enough as I stand here on my own. Luke hadn't wanted to come with me either. I told him about the rock pools on the beach and I offered to help him fish, but he'd shaken his head and snuggled closer to Mum. Her hand was inside his T-shirt and she was rubbing his back as they lazed close together on the patio after lunch. Last week he had been disappointed when we got home from school and she wasn't there. They were making up for lost time, I suppose. They looked up and waved when I said goodbye. Mum told me to have a good time, then she blew on Luke's pink cheek and he giggled and squirmed with delight all over again.

The beach was only a walk away from Gran's old house, but from our new one, here, I have to take the bus. I've written the times down because I can't miss the last one back. I wish I'd brought something to drink. The sun is intense through the glass. I'm the only passenger and we wind through the hot, high-banked lanes until we reach the last stop.

I climb the stile and jump down into the grass. It's very, very quiet. There are blackberry bushes growing in low clumps. I pick some berries and eat them slowly, crushing the pips between my teeth.

I can't believe how small everything has become, the stile and the wall are low and nothing out of the ordinary at all. Climbing them, then, on my own, had been such a big deal. I think I'd even kicked out at Tom and told him to leave me alone when he'd tried to help. But the path hasn't changed, nor the smell of thyme and mint, and the red dust still scratches between my toes.

Further on I pause and look around. Something has changed. The approach to the beach is not as I remember it and I can't make it out. Then I understand: they've put in steps. Instead of the long scramble down, with the earth rubbed so smooth in some places that you couldn't help but slide, now there are proper steps. They are on the far side of a rocky outcrop, cut into the cliff and edged with wood like thick doorstep sandwiches. I stand at the top and look down. There's a halfway seat where the steps turn around. It's new too, and unscratched, with its varnish and brass plate still bright in the sun. The legs are sunk in a plinth of white concrete and it reminds me of a seaside throne. If I wasn't all on my own I'd have sat there for a bit, but you need a friend for that, so I put my foot on the first step and begin to walk down.

There would have been space enough for both Tom and me, side by side on those steps, and I know what we'd have done. We'd have held hands, with my shoulder bumping his chest and both of us putting the same foot forward each time. We did that a lot. We'd have run faster and faster until, at the bottom, he'd have been holding me up, saving me from skidding flat on my bum into the rabble of shingle and driftwood and rubbish heaped there by the sea.

Alone, I don't run. I go down, step by step, and then jump on to the bank of pebbles at the bottom. Some dislodge and roll on, but I stand still. This is how it was: the ends and bits of bright rope, orange and green and blue, that have come back from the sea, the bundles of buried nets and the tattered gulls' feathers and soft-edged bits of coloured glass that I used to collect. I squat on the shingle and gouge some pebbles out. I find the cool wetness deep down as I push my fingers in between.

The beach is quite deserted. I hadn't expected that. I'd imagined children at least, playing along the water's edge. It's Saturday after all, but there's no one here except me. The tide is a long way out but in the middle of the beach the Red Rock still rises up. Far beyond it, tankers are anchored in the bay, and beyond them a white sail moves slowly across.

The pool will have been uncovered by this low tide. Now, if I walk down and lean over, I'll see my face amongst the swaying fronds and yellow bands of weed and I'll see the reflection of the Red Rock above.

I take off my sandals and walk towards it over the sand. It's still impossibly high and sheer and the pool below is still too small, and I'm glad. Up on the cliff I'd wondered if I'd made a mistake about that too. I'd worried that the dive had never been anything special, and was just some kid's thing after all. I was wrong. It terrifies me still.

I half close my eyes against the sun and I look up at the Red Rock. There are trails of seaweed hanging from it, and shells and stones jammed in its trickling cracks. It's almost warm to touch and the slanting white lines of other strata are clamped between like cut-through fat in a slab of dark red meat. Way above me, on the edge, is the place where he stood.

'*He-len*!'

It *was* my name, although no one is about.

Then there's a blast on a car horn. A 'toot–to–to–toot'. It's a ridiculous sound so I can't be imagining it and anyway the white van never sounded its horn. All the witnesses agreed that the only sound was a squeal of brakes.

'*He-len*! Over here!'

Then I see a car. It must have gone over the edge of the cliff some time ago, but slowly, if that's possible, because it's wrecked though not smashed to bits. It's nose down amongst the boulders on the far side of the beach. The orange bonnet is buckled and sticking up. The doors hang like broken arms. The windows have shattered and the tyres are burst but it's still a car. And the horn must work. Now I can see Wiffy Owens hunched over the wheel. He sounds the horn again and beckons to me through the empty windscreen.

'I knew you'd come,' he shouts as I wander across. 'I've been waiting.'

The seats are ripped and the metalwork is bright with powdering rust. I can't think how I missed it as I came down the steps.

'You want to sit in too?' Wiffy asks.

'Not really, but thanks. Has it been here long?'

'I don't know. But I'm the only one who uses it now, so it's mine, isn't it, in a way? And yours, if you like, Helen.'

I look at the rust and the split radiator half buried in the

48

sand and I don't know what to say. Pebbles and seaweed and shells and bits of wood have piled up and the next winter storm might bury the wreck altogether but Wiffy doesn't seem to care. He fiddles with the steering wheel and makes a noise like changing gear. I walk away towards the Red Rock but he follows and touches my arm.

'So you never found them,' he blinks rapidly and his eye slides.

'Found what?'

'My matches, my little box of matches that you took from me and then lost.'

'Of course I haven't!' I stare at him. So, he does remember after all. In one stroke, he's torn off the intervening years like skin.

'It doesn't matter,' he mutters as though he's excusing me for some mistake.

'For heaven's sake, Wiffy, that was years ago and I didn't lose them on purpose, did I?' I'm angry with him and he's standing too close. Even for a dumb kid who still thinks that a stupid box of matches can buy him what he wants, he's still too close.

'Anyway, what do you want matches for?' I sit down on a jutting rock.

'To light fires, of course.'

'But why do you want to light fires?'

'Because it's nice,' he sits down too and slides across.

'So you're like Prometheus!'

'Yes!' He leaps round. 'How did you know that?'

It was a stupid comment. I had said it to show off, and to put him off, because he is still shoving his skinny knee against mine. I was sure he wouldn't know who Prometheus was. I only know because Greek myths and legends were one of Tom's passions. He wanted to be an archaeologist

49

and had lots of books about the Ancient Greeks. They were in his bedroom in our old house and I used to look at the pictures. His books haven't been unpacked because he doesn't have a room here. Mum and Dad never said anything to me about it, so I don't bring it up. It just happened. There are four bedrooms in this house and, with Gran moved in, they're full. There's no room for Tom.

'Fancy you knowing about Prometheus!' Wiffy's face is close to mine.

'Of course I know! He was the Greek God of Fire and –'

'No, he wasn't!'

'Oh.'

'*Hephaestus* was God of Fire. Prometheus *stole* fire from Mount Olympus to put life into a little clay man he'd made, but Zeus punished him because fire can only belong to the Gods.' He speaks very fast.

'Oh.' I'm annoyed. Wiffy Owens has wrong-footed me and I don't like that.

'That's why Zeus chained Prometheus to the rock and sent this bird, this vulture down – you know about vultures?' He looks at me pityingly.

'Get on with it, Wiffy!' I scowl. He's boring me now and I recognize his sort. There was one in my tutor group at my old school, a geeky boy called Pete who memorized pages and pages of figures about trains but couldn't make sense of anything else. If you asked Pete anything simple like 'how are you?' he never answered. Pat sometimes talked to him and if she'd been here she'd probably have known what to say to Wiffy. I don't. I just scowl.

'And this vulture pecks out Prometheus' liver as a punishment,' Wiffy is watching me closely, 'but the wound heals over, so every day the vulture can start again and peck and peck.'

'Shut up, Wiffy! Lay off, can't you?'

'And peck . . . and peck . . . and peck!' He's picked up a small, sharp piece of driftwood and is pretending to stab the Red Rock.

His mouth is open and a fleck of saliva flies from his lips. I turn my back on him and make for the steps. He calls out but I don't stop. When I get to the seat, he's still flinging himself back and forth across the stones. He seems to have forgotten about me, but as I'm getting my breath back at the top his chant echoes up. I suddenly wonder if he pushed that car over the cliff himself. He's such a nutter that it could have been his idea of fun.

I'm panting after running up the steps, which shows how out of condition I am. I begin to walk more slowly towards the stile. It's early for the bus but I might as well wait. There's nothing else to do except turn round for one more look. A gull is still drifting overhead and the tankers are still anchored in the silent, silver bay but the white sail has gone. Then I turn back. I step off the grass into the rougher, thicker growth of gorse and low, dense bush that leads to the edge of the cliff. The sun is very hot on the back of my neck and the air is thick and still. I look behind me quickly, but I'm entirely alone. This is where the old path should have been, if wind and rain and a fall of rocky, red earth hadn't scoured it clean. This is where Tom and I had run, going faster and faster and always hand in hand. Now there's no way down.

I ease myself forward, inch by inch, until I'm lying flat. Then I look over the edge. I fasten my hands amongst the roots and clumps of pinks in the dry, crumbling earth and I can almost see him again, almost feel his hand grasping mine as we slither down and jump, finally, on to the ringing pebble ridge.

51

Then I smell burning. Wiffy must have set the pile of driftwood alight. The smoke is floating up on the warm evening air and it catches my throat while, nearby, something moves. I lie perfectly still and I know that someone is there. I press my face into the brittle spikes of sea grass as they tread towards me. They are pushing their way through and coming nearer and nearer, so I turn my head.

A man is standing about ten metres away peering through binoculars at the sea. He takes a few more steps through the gorse then looks again and there's no escape. Slowly, from side to side, he's examining the bay. There's nothing I can do, because he will catch sight of me in the end, so I lie there, with my face in the grass, and I wish I could just die.

'I'm sorry,' he says. 'I didn't see you there. For heaven's sake be careful!' A crust of soil breaks off as I sit up and pebbles ring and bounce as they ricochet down. Christian Owens holds out his hand but I don't take it. I just wriggle back like some great worm until I'm on the path.

'I didn't mean to startle you but I had a message. Someone has seen something so I had to come out and look for myself.'

'I know,' I say quickly, 'I've already seen him.'

'What? Where?'

'Down there,' I point over the edge. 'He's down there and he's lit a fire, it's driftwood and that's what you can smell.'

'You mean *Wiffy*'s on the beach?'

'Yes.'

'Oh well,' he laughs nervously, 'that's all right then, isn't it? I needn't have bothered.' He glances back at the sea and I suddenly realize that Christian Owens hasn't been looking for Wiffy at all.

'But you really shouldn't do that,' he smiles at me now.

'Do what?'

52

'Go so near the edge. Should you?'

I shrug because I don't know what to say. We begin to walk back across the grass but at the wall I take his hand and let him help me down.

Chapter 7

'He only gave me a lift back!' I'm using the phone in the hall and Mum's in the kitchen so I need to take care. 'That's all, Pat.'

'Is it?' she asks after a long pause.

'Yes! And why shouldn't I drive back with him? Since he offered and since we're practically neighbours? His family lives in this row of houses I pass on the way to school. And he works with Mum at the garden centre. He told me so.'

There's another silence. That's the trouble with long-distance calls. When Pat was only a few streets away we could have as many silences as we needed. Now, when these calls are so expensive, it feels as if we must keep on talking. Suddenly she laughs. I imagine her lying flat on her back on her double bed. She'll be wearing her black jeans and her bare feet will be moving around as if she wants to be running in air. She's laughing at me devilishly, her stomach shaking, and the phone fluttering in her hand.

'Go *on*, Helen,' she gurgles. 'Just spit it out. What's the guy *like*?'

'Well, nothing special. Honestly! His name's Christian Owens and he's the brother, the older brother of this odd kid in my tutor group. And –'

'What's the odd kid's name?'

'Wiffy. Wiffy Owens, and he's obsessed with Greek myths. He thinks –'

'Stop avoiding the issue, Helen. I want to hear about *your* bloke.'

'He's not *my* bloke!' I glance towards the kitchen. 'Honestly, Pat. He only gave me a lift home. I met him on the cliffs above our beach. You remember the beach, where the Red Rock was? Well, yesterday I went back there and this guy practically trod on me.'

'*Helen*!'

'Not like *that*! I was trying to see over the edge of the cliff and he was there too. That's all.'

'Where?'

'Pat, just shut up and listen.'

'OK.'

She does and I hear rustling as she nestles the phone into the pillow beside her ear. She'll be smiling as she waits for my story. She knows that I fall for guys but never do anything about it. I'm a wimp and only worship from afar. I wonder if she remembers this boy who started getting on our bus in the mornings. I thought he was gorgeous, and I wasn't the only one. Everybody said he was cute. All the girls started getting seats by themselves on the top deck in the hope that he'd sit beside them. One day, when Pat missed the bus and I was on my own, he sat beside me. I nearly died. I know it's pathetic but I was *so* excited and he never even spoke to me, never even glanced at me, but I still died. I told Pat and we discussed him but I didn't tell her how I'd felt. I was embarrassed, even with her. I hadn't known that you could feel like that about a total stranger. Secretly, I used to pretend that he had actually spoken to me but I never got anywhere because I couldn't decide what he was likely to say. Sad, aren't I? Murray! Murray-something, that was his name.

I imagine her lying on her bed waiting for me to continue. Her strange coloured hair will be spread out on the pillow. It's not fair like mine, or ginger, but truly reddish gold. All the Rook girls have it. They're a striking lot. Pat's freckly too, and the marks are touched on to her pale skin like stippling on a fish, but it's attractive. If she hadn't been a runner, she'd have been a brilliant swimmer or diver, and a champion at that.

'Well?' she prompts at last.

'Well, he's not bad.' I take a deep breath. 'Actually Pat, he's the sort of bloke who makes your feet feel soft and your toes curl under.'

'That good? Steady on, Helen.'

'No! Honestly. And what's more, he *looks* exactly like a pirate. He's sunburnt, and you can see the line where the tan stops on the back of his neck. Then the skin's white. And he always wears this old red sweater thing.'

'And?'

'And shorts, *old* shorts. His legs are . . . well, he's very tall. Much taller than me, so over six foot, at least.'

'Perfect. Fair or dark?'

'Fair, I think, but sort of in between. It's hard to say, because he is so sunburnt and his hair's quite long and untidy. And he's got a boat.'

'A *boat*! Well, he'd have to, wouldn't he? You don't get many pirates walking on water. What's the boat called?'

'The *Black Pig*. It's a fishing boat, but I think it belongs to his father. And that's another thing, the father's missing. At sea.'

'How awful. Do you know what happened?'

'No. I just read about it in the local newspaper. Christian didn't mention it on the drive back. Nor did the younger brother, Wiffy. No, the only one who's said anything is the sister, Samantha. She's in the year above, and one day last week she couldn't stop crying in school, so they sent for me! Because of "Life Long", that's why.'

56

'Oh, Helen, that's not fair. I'm so sorry.'

'I know. And it's partly my fault because I should have refused, but I didn't. So that's how I met Samantha and do you know what she said? She said, "I wish I'd done it myself."'

'Oh dear,' Pat's voice is careful. 'That does not sound good. But what about this Christian? Didn't he say anything?'

'Not a word. But he's really nice, Pat. Like a brother. And kind.'

'You fancy him, Helen Kopperberg!'

'I don't! But even if I did, he's too old. He's –'

'Helen! For goodness sake, love.' Mum puts her head round the door. 'You've been on that phone for hours. Suppose somebody else is trying to get through?'

'Sorry.' Mum's right and I feel a bit guilty. 'Look, Pat, I've got to go.'

'OK then. Bye. And love to everyone, Helen.'

When she's gone I miss her even more. Upstairs Luke will be sound asleep. In the kitchen Mum is still putting things away. Gran's watching telly; this morning she picked more roses and filled the vase on the telephone table. They've opened and as I sit in the darkening hall I smell their golden perfume and it reminds me of other summers, and the scent of summer nights.

In our other house, when I was little and couldn't sleep because it was too hot or too light, I'd lie awake in the endless, restless dusk. I'd listen to the evening sounds drifting in from the recreation ground and I'd smell the roses. Sometimes, after the council workers had been mowing, I could smell the sharp, green sap of cut-off grass as well. I played in the recreation ground a lot but by six o'clock we younger children went home. After a final slide or another slow spin on the old roundabout whose chipped, red paint was warm and sticky to touch, I'd have to wave goodbye.

57

Other children who were braver or luckier than me would look up from the sand-pit and wave back. I'd squeeze through the bent railings and run fast up the twitten and round the corner to the black and white house where a dog barked. I was afraid of Dandy. He was big and hairy and he stood up against the curly iron gate at the side of that house. He barked shrilly, and his claws scrabbled and scraped against the metal.

I'd tiptoe past so he wouldn't notice, then I could hop-scotch the rest of the way. Once, when it was hot and sticky, I saw flying ants. Streams of them flew up from the cracks in the paving slabs and I hopped straight into them. When I reached our garden I was covered, and even had them in my mouth.

Our garden was all right, but it wasn't anything special. The rockery was nice in spring, and I liked the cherry tree a lot, but compared to our next-door neighbour's garden it was nothing. An old lady lived there and that garden was special. In summer her roses perfumed the whole street.

That's what I could smell as I lay awake: their sweet scent mixed with the green of the grass and, as the light faded, I began to hear the rippling voices of the older ones who inherited the playground when we kids had all gone home to bed.

Some adults protested about the teenagers. They wanted to keep them out of the playground. They started petitions and mothers stood around with placards but it never did any good. The playground was always full of them in the evenings.

They never did much except sit about. The evenings would start off with all the girls on one piece of equipment and all the boys on another. The girls would swing slowly and sometimes I'd hear the creak of the chains. The boys fooled around on the climbing frame, doing monkey calls

58

and pull-ups and scratching their armpits. Then they'd begin to move around. They'd chase each other in and out. Later, as the light slid away, they would begin to split into couples. That's what the adults didn't like. When Tom started going there in the evenings I asked him about it and he said that the couples kissed, and did stuff like that. I was curious, I remember that. Mum and Dad didn't like him going, but he still went.

Occasionally I'd creep into his room when I knew he was out. His window always had the better view. I wanted to see him 'kissing and doing stuff like that'. But I never did. I only smelt the roses and heard voices in the dark.

Then, a few days after he'd died, Gran and I left the house for the first time. I think we had to buy something or post a letter. We walked hand in hand down our road and past the rose garden. It was different but I didn't understand why. When I looked back, I saw that all the wonderful flowers were gone. Gran told me that the old lady had gone out that same evening and cut everything, cut all the best and most beautiful blooms and taken them to the spot where Tom had died. I never saw her roses there, but that's what Gran said, and she held my hand so tightly that I couldn't hop. I asked Gran why the garden had been spoilt. I didn't understand that Tom was dead. I thought it was a shame to have cut everything like that.

'Helen! What are you doing in the dark?' Gran comes out of the sitting room. She and Dad have been watching the news.

'Nothing. Just sitting.'

'Rubbish!' Mum puts her head round the door. 'Helen's been wearing that phone out talking to Pat.' She leans in the doorway, her arms folded. She's still wearing her garden centre T-shirt. It makes her look younger and I know she likes that. She's sunburnt too and it suits her.

'Well go on, Helen. What are those mad Rooks up to now?' Mum smiles.

'I didn't ask! How awful. I just rabbited on about me. And about us.'

Mum is rubbing hand cream into her fingers. She's taking care of herself again and I'm glad.

'I hope you told them that we're all all right,' she smiles. 'That we're settling in just fine. Because we are, aren't we?'

Before we can answer Luke cries out. I bound up the stairs to his room. The poor lamb must have got overheated because he's drenched in sweat. I open another window and push back the tidal wave of soft animals which he insists on sleeping under. I smooth down his damp hair and kiss his hot cheek. He mutters something but doesn't wake. Sometimes, in the other house, I used to slip into bed beside him. I used to lie on my side with my knees under his warm little bum and my nose amongst his thistledown hair. But he's older now and he pushes me away, so this evening I only kiss him and go back down.

'You should have watched the news,' Gran is excited, 'it was local and very interesting. They even showed the dock.'

'That's right.' Dad joins us in the hall. He's yawning, stretching one arm above his head, patting his hand to and fro over his opened mouth. 'We've made the headlines, at long last. It was about that boat, the *Black Pig*. It was about old David Owens: it seems that they still haven't found his body, yet.'

Chapter 8

'What about it?' I ask, trying to keep my voice indifferent and still.

'The news said that the boat had been taken into dock by the police! Our moment of fame, or infamy, depending on how you look at it. But there was a great shot of the dock and the Point.' Dad smiles. 'If the camera had stayed on a moment longer, I'd have seen our house! But we saw the *Black Pig*. I should think the authorities are going over it with a fine-tooth comb. And that son of his –'

'Christian!' interrupts Gran. 'Christian! As soon as I hear it, I'm thinking oh no! Don't let a good name like that belong to someone who is so wicked!'

'Wicked?' Mum steps out of the doorway. 'Whatever do you mean?'

'You don't call it wicked, to kill a father?' Gran is sharp.

'What!' Mum shouts back.

I don't understand what is happening. Why are the four of us suddenly facing one another like gladiators in the ring? Mum draws a quick breath, but I get in first.

'And what *about* Christian?' I ask. 'What's it got to do with him?'

'Well?' Mum moves to the table, beside me and opposite them. 'Well? Wouldn't you like to explain? Since you two seem to know all about it.'

'There's nothing to explain, Juliet.' Dad is fed up. 'It's just local news. The boat is being examined by the police and this young fellow, the son, is helping them with their

61

inquiries. That's all. I only mentioned it because they're a local family. Mother and I know them from way back. And since Christian is obviously involved –'

'He *isn't* involved!' Mum and I speak at exactly the same moment.

Dad looks up.

'He's the young fellow at the garden centre, the one I told you about. The one who knew Tom,' Mum is gripping the edge of the table. 'He's a part-timer, does some of the heavy outdoor work when he isn't at sea, and does it well, too! That's how *I* know he isn't "wicked" let alone "involved". He's a nice lad.'

They all look at me.

'I saw him once, on the way to school, and his brother's in my tutor group. Luke and I saw him, saw them *both*, one morning last week. That's all I meant.'

They are still looking at me.

'So what?' I demand. 'What's so special about Christian Owens?'

'Nothing. It's just the family,' Dad yawns. 'They always were a bad lot. I've known David since we were kids. We went to school together, when he turned up, that is. Everybody round here knows David Owens and his family, so when you hear that the police are questioning one of them, you put two and two together. It's a small place, down here.'

'You're telling me! "A bad lot",' Mum mimics Dad's tone. 'Honestly, Charles, you should hear yourself. Talk about giving a dog a bad name!' She isn't being fair. Dad never gives a dog a bad name. Unlike Gran.

'They are criminals, those Owens,' Gran frowns, 'and thieves. They always were. Families like that never change. It is like disease in a family, they pass it on.'

'Rubbish!' Mum snorts, but there's no stopping Gran.

'So Helen, you must take care. Like your father says, it is a small place you are in. And the people talk.'

'That's complete rubbish!' Mum explodes.

'It isn't rubbish, Juliet. Even in Holland, we had such families, even in a good neighbourhood like ours. And in the war . . .' She stops and shakes her head. 'Never mind that now. You don't want to hear about that, Juliet, and you don't know the world like I do. And thank God. You don't know what people can do.'

'Don't I?'

Mum's voice drags back all the old bitterness and grief and suddenly I'm angry too. Why can't Gran keep quiet? Won't she ever shut up about what happened to her in the war? Or give up her crown of thorns? Recently Mum's been doing well, so much better. And I want her like that, with a sunburnt nose and lipstick and a smile. I reach for her hand and I massage in a smear of the cream around her thumb.

'Heavens, Gran,' I try a joke, 'you'll be telling us next that the Owens are pirates! Have they got peg legs and parrots and patches over their eyes?'

'Actually, you're dead right, Helen,' Dad joins in eagerly. 'The old boy, old Jack Owens, David's father, did have an eyepatch! It was black, with an elastic over his head! So you can guess what we kids called him behind his back?'

'No. What?'

'Pirate Jack, of course! Though we made sure he never heard us.'

'That's right,' Gran is not smiling, 'but he was *not* a pirate. A rough man, certainly, but not a pirate. That I know for sure, because he told me.'

'Just listen to yourselves!' Mum pulls her hand from mine. 'Can't any of you *ever* let anything drop? Are you

63

going to condemn the grandson because you didn't like the grandfather's face?'

'Hang on, Juliet.' Dad tries, but Mum won't listen. She runs up the stairs and we hear the bedroom door shut.

Gran sighs. Dad taps his teeth. He mutters something about there being reasons why the police question people, then he yawns again, and opens his office door. There's a fizz as his computer screen flickers back to life.

As soon as Gran has gone upstairs I go into the kitchen and begin to rifle through the newspaper pile. I examine it twice but the paper with black shoe polish marks and the article about the Owens isn't there.

The kitchen door is wide open. Mum's tidied up but forgotten that. A handful of moths has fluttered in to drum against the light. I glance towards the sea. The moon is so bright that I can see right to the bottom of the garden. I can even see the bushes by the fence. That's why Luke couldn't sleep. Outside it could be day.

Only it isn't and it isn't moonlight either. As I step on to the patio, I see the flame. A thick red flag of rolling flame leaps from one of the chimney stacks on the refinery opposite. It's huge. I've never seen anything like it. Sea, shore and sky are lit up by its glow. The moon is there, but drifting white and disregarded amongst clouds.

When I stand still I can even hear the flame. A night wind blows off the water and with it comes a gusting, gushing rush that must be the sound of fire. It's colouring everything and its reflection is flung down on to the sea which glistens and shifts like shot, black silk. The jetty, the tankers, the masts of yachts moored in the bay glow as if they are all red hot.

It makes me think of volcanoes and the molten, moving centre of the earth and war. Wasn't there a missile that flew through the door of an underground bunker in Baghdad?

Didn't it burn up all the women and children sheltering down there? Pat talked about these things a lot. She and her father are pacifists, so whenever war cropped up in class she always tried to have her say. I watch the flame in the sky. There were three little brothers, weren't there, in Northern Ireland, about a year ago. They were burnt to death in their own home with the flames underneath and no way out. I watch it surge and wave. You can imagine it scorching the underside of clouds. And it couldn't be much fun for a cormorant or sea bird, which flew too close. That'd be it, wouldn't it? The great bird crematorium in the sky!

That's what they did to Tom. On the day of his funeral, dressed in too many clothes for a warm afternoon and standing between Dad and Gran, I didn't understand where the golden wooden box with its lid of flowers, was going. Music started, *his* music that he'd played all that summer and as it played the coffin slid away between blue curtains, which swished. The flowers were still on top, including the special cushion of daisies that had my name on it, and though I knew it was a coffin, I didn't believe that Tom was in it. And I didn't understand what was going to happen. Later, when I understood about crematoriums, I didn't like it at all. How could they? That's what I thought, though I never said. How *could* they have done that to Tom?

If he hadn't died, he'd have probably left home by now. He'd have gone to university like Pat's sisters, and shared a flat with his mates. He wanted to be an archaeologist so he'd have gone abroad on digs, and I'd have hardly seen him, or only now and then. He'd already started going away. The local history society was excavating something Roman that the motorway extension had uncovered and he was there a lot. He even had his own museum in our garden shed. He'd started it when he was very young and I'd sold hand-made tickets to friends and family. He'd written out little labels for all the exhibits and I thought it was brilliant.

I haven't seen that stuff for ages and I haven't thought about it for years. I'll have to ask Dad. They couldn't have chucked it out. Tom was proud of his collection of jaws. Some had curled, yellow teeth which I used to rattle like castanets and he didn't mind. He had bits of earthenware pots and slim, white stems from old clay pipes. There was a collection of small, thick glass bottles which were Victorian, I think. He'd dug them out of a bank on the common. I'd helped with that, and carried the earth away in a bucket and tipped it in a ditch.

All his things must be somewhere, still hidden away. They'll be in one of those boxes which Mum won't unpack. She couldn't have got rid of them. Not her.

I go back inside, lock the kitchen door and feel my way quietly through the house into the garage. A pile of boxes is stacked against one wall. I slit the thick brown tape with the edge of a chisel. And there they are, in the second box, as if I knew all along. It isn't his museum exhibits, but at least it's his books. Their covers feel cold and dusty and the pages on this one have been bent back. I take it out and gently open it up.

'For big brother Tom, Love from Mum and Dad. 12 May 1985.' *My* birthday, but not *my* book. It's a present to him on the day I was born: so the *Just William* book was never mine, and I hadn't noticed! Did they buy a copy for me later, because I loved the stories so much? Or did Tom give me his copy? No wonder he knew it by heart when he sat on the edge of my bed. I pull out another, then pause, then quickly put it back. Someone has got up in the house above. I wait until it's quiet and safe and then I relax.

That's his stamp album, and those are some clothes and a

pair of trainers, and at the bottom more books. I recognize the cover of one of them. It's Helios, the Sun God, riding across the sky in his chariot. I liked that picture a lot when I was little, especially the four winged horses. If I remember correctly, there were loads of animal pictures in this book and pictures of people with no clothes on. When I looked at them on my own, I used to stare at the naked bodies of Hercules and Aphrodite and wonder how it would be when I was grown-up, like that.

Prometheus is in the index, on page 57. I shut the box and take the book up to my room. I can't quite read the words by the light of the flame but as I sit by the window it illuminates the pictures well enough. Anyway, that's how it must have been in ancient times. Those people must have looked at their gods by the yellow guttering flames of oil or rush lamps. They'd have smelt burning just like me and seen the shifting shadows and the trails of smoke.

I stop at the marble statue of Hercules. I remember it well. He's resting after one of the Seven Labours and leaning on the massive, knotted trunk of tree which he used as a club. You can see his muscles like slabs of rock and the veins snaking up over his belly from the curled pubic hair. A lion's head is impaled on the club and the rest of its skin hangs down like a cloak; its mouth is open and you can see the fangs, even though the shut eyes are dead. The picture frightened me as a child.

I'm still surprised that Wiffy Owens knew about stuff like this. I can't imagine that family having any books in the house especially after what Dad said. I wasn't even sure if Wiffy could read. The teachers never ask him and I've seen him pushing his finger along a line only to have it stranded mid-page as the class ploughs on ahead. Greek myths can't mean anything to him. Even I find the names difficult and I like books and reading.

67

Still, there's no reason why I shouldn't lend this to him. He might be interested. Who knows? If he isn't in school tomorrow, I could drop the book off at their house. I could say hello to him and Sam, and if Christian just happened to be there, I could say hello to him too.

I've been thinking about what Mum said. It must be so awful for him and Sam to have people gossiping about them like that. For all of them, I suppose. I can't imagine what it must feel like to have people suggesting that you're responsible for the death of one of your family and I don't want to think about it at all.

Outside the flame has died. I can barely see, so I get into bed. I switch on my bedside light and snuggle up. Wiffy has missed a bit out, or maybe he never knew. It wasn't only the theft of fire that made Zeus so mad. Prometheus' brother was to blame too. He rejected Zeus's special gift of a woman and that finally made the god lose his rag. That's when he sent the vulture down, to torment Prometheus each day anew. I bet Wiffy doesn't know about Pandora. That was the woman's name. She was the most enchanting woman in the world and she opened the box. She was the one who was cursed for letting trouble out among men. I bet Wiffy Owens doesn't know this. And he should, with a sister like Sam.

Chapter 9

'Over here, Helen!' Wiffy starts as soon as I've picked up my tray. 'I've saved you a place. Don't sit there, sit *here*, by me. This is *your* place, Helen. I've been keeping it for you. *Helen*, you've got to sit here!' People look up from their plates and snigger.

'"Oh Helen, darling Helen, you've just *got* to sit by *me*",' a boy opposite mimics. The giggling spreads.

'Or *on* me!' another voice prompts. 'Oh, yes! Yes! Yes! Sit on me, Helen Copperbottom, sit on me and squash me flat! Trample me, Helen, and I'll love every minute!' The speaker chokes on his own laughter.

I want to disappear. This has been going on all week and it's my fault. I've gone so red I must be purple.

'Helen?' Wiffy points as though I could have possibly missed either him or the place he's been keeping free.

Tomorrow I'm not going to eat lunch. I'm never coming in here again. I'm never going to sit down with those blokes. They're pigs, nothing but pigs in ties, with their spotty, whiskery snouts in the trough and bits of food dropped down their shirt fronts. I hate them but I hate myself more because I started all this.

Last Monday afternoon, when Wiffy wasn't in school, I did what I'd planned. I took Tom's book of Greek myths and knocked on the Owens' front door. I even waited when nobody answered and I knocked again. I kept on knocking until, finally, a door opened somewhere and steps shuffled down uncarpeted stairs. I should have gone even then, but

I didn't. I left it too late.

'Yes?' The front door opened a crack. 'Who is it?'

'It's Helen . . . it's . . . I'm Helen . . .'

'Helen?' A woman's voice wearily tried out my name. 'Helen? One of Sam's friends, are you?' The door opened just wide enough for me to see that Mrs Owens was still in her nightdress and slippers.

'Not really. I'm Wiffy's . . . Wiffy's . . .'

Sylvia Owens screamed his name.

'Wiffy! Come on up, Wiff!' She let fall the torn edges of the pink nightie and she screamed again. 'Wiffy! Come here, can't you?'

'It's only this book, Mrs Owens. It's for Wiffy.' I felt so stupid: she'd just lost her husband and I was fussing about a book of Greek myths.

'Wi – ffy!'

Was she mad? You could have heard that scream at the end of the street.

'I just thought Wiffy might be interested. It was my brother's.' I took a step back, but it was too late. Christian Owens was coming up the path.

'It's Wiff's girl, Christian.'

'Oh, no! I'm not, I'm –'

'She's come round for him. Isn't that nice? And she's brought him something. What is it, dear? A book?' She turned it over and over as if she wasn't quite sure. 'I've called Wiffy, but he doesn't seem to have heard. Maybe you could have a go, could you? Give him another shout. Tell him his young lady's here! I could put the kettle on, couldn't I? Should I do that, Christian?' Something of pleasure softened her gaunt face and that's why I stayed when I should have gone.

Christian bent down and knocked sharply on the floor in the hall.

70

'Wiffy? You down there, boy?'

A trap door in the hall floor suddenly lifted up and made me jump.

'Helen!' Wiffy cried, as he clambered out. 'You've come!'

'Wiffy,' Christian's voice was stern and Wiffy looked away. 'You turned the light off, down there, Wiff?' Christian looked at me. 'He gets muddled about things, does Wiffy, but I expect you've noticed that, haven't you Helen?'

I didn't answer him because I didn't know what to say.

Mrs Owens made tea but Christian took his mug outside. He said he had things to do. That left the three of us, sitting too close around a dirty kitchen table. Mrs Owens didn't say anything and Wiffy didn't have to. He drank his tea but his eyes never left my face. From then on he's never left my side and I think I'll go mad. 'Wiff's got it bad,' Mandy said yesterday. She's one of the girls I talk to a bit. 'You want to watch out, Helen. He'll follow you into the loo, given half a chance.'

She's right. Everyone's noticed but they're all laughing at me, not him. I'm the idiot. I'm the one who can't tell Wiffy Owens to get lost.

'Trample you, Phil?' Samantha's voice cuts through the lunchtime row like a crack in glass. 'You must be joking! Who'd want to do that and get their nice clean shoes covered in crap? Now shut up, Phil Thomas, before I tip this down your neck!' She's holding her tray over him and she lets it tilt. 'Shut up, Phil, and shove up. *I* want to sit down too.'

Phil shrugs, and shifts along. Sam slams down her tray and waits. Phil glances sideways at me, shrugs again and gets up to make space, but grins.

I know it's only a dumb joke, even the Copperbottom bit. Phil and his mates like a laugh. Who doesn't? I should have joined in, then plonked myself on his lap. That's what Pat

71

would have done. She'd have flung herself on him, then bounced up and down going, 'Yes! Yes! Yes!', like the woman in that film. She'd have kept on until the guy was crimson with embarrassment. That would have been Pat's way. Only it's not mine. I can't. I smile miserably at Sam and climb into the space they've made but I'm thinking of escape.

I skive off games and go in search of Mrs Cable. I'm surprised at how easily I lie and how willingly she believes me. She says she's sorry and she reaches up and lays her hand on my forehead. She agrees that I do feel too hot. Am I sickening for flu? Or something else? I tell her that my grandmother has been ill all week.

'Well, Helena, it could be that, couldn't it, dear? And it's always better to be safe than sorry, especially at this time of year. Now, would you like to stay in the warm?' We both glance through the white sickroom window. Grey drizzle is beginning to fall on the playing fields outside. 'Or you can go home, Helena, if that's what you want?'

I don't want to do either but I don't tell her that.

She gives me permission to leave and I grab my jacket as quickly as I can.

I walk briskly from the hoarse voices on the football pitch and the flat, wet thud of netballs. Soon I can't hear any school sounds at all. Dark grey clouds are massing overhead. It's not cold but wind is curling round the corners of the terrace houses and tossing the gulls so that they tilt and wheel. I hurry into the primary school.

'Helen!' Luke breaks free from a line of small children. Ignoring his teacher's cry, he shoots across the playground. 'Helen! I didn't know you were meeting me.' He fastens himself to my hand.

'I wasn't. But I thought it'd be nice. They let us out early.' I squeeze his hand.

'What? *All* of you?' He looks anxiously up the street, as though he expects the whole comprehensive to be following me.

'No, no. Just *me*. As a treat. Is that all right?' He nods eagerly. 'So we could do something, go somewhere, if you like?' He doesn't answer. 'You could show me your class-room. Do you have any paintings up?'

'No.'

'Or stars? I bet you've got heaps of gold stars.' He always had stars in his old school. He liked me to go in and count them and be amazed.

He doesn't answer, so I suppose it isn't such a big deal now he's older.

'Helen! Come on!' He jerks at my hand. I catch his teacher's eye. She frowns irritably but mouths 'yes', and as the bell rings Luke is the first kid out of the gate.

Suddenly it comes on to rain heavily. The wind blows fat drops and yellow leaves from the branches of the trees. My toes are beginning to squish in my right shoe. I must have sprung a leak. Luke smiles up at me like a small, wet water-rat. His hair is plastered down. My shirt is sticking and we're both soaked through but without a word we veer off towards the cliffs and the long way round.

'Left!' I call. 'Left, left, left!' We march in time, swinging our arms and not breaking step, even when it lands us in the middle of a puddle and the water splashes up. Luke laughs and so do I. The waterway is dim and grey with rain, but I stop near the Point.

'Come on,' Luke drags on my hand but I don't move until I'm sure that the *Black Pig* isn't there. The passenger ferry passes on its way to Ireland. Luke waves but there's no one standing at the rails today. No one waves back so we march on, stamping and splashing as hard as we can.

73

'Good heavens!' Dad sees us from the kitchen window and opens the back door. 'What's all this about?' He shakes his head as we stand and drip. 'I could have collected you if you'd phoned.'

Luke stretches out his tongue and licks a drop from the tip of his nose. 'I *love* rain!' He's jumping around, making muddy footprints and shaking himself so that the water spins off.

'Hey!' Dad snatches up the kitchen towel and wraps it tight around to hold him fast. 'Steady on, old man.' He's kissing Luke, cradling him in his arms and nuzzling the top of his head through the damp striped towel.

I go upstairs. The stitching on my shoe is split. When I feel inside the toe my fingers go through. Hopefully tomorrow will be dry. I pull off my things. On that foot my toes are navy blue! So much for shoe polish. My skirt is damp and splashed with mud so I put it over the back of my chair. There are still scabs on my knees. I'd wear trousers to school but when you're as big as me you can easily look as if you've stepped into a couple of black tents. Even my bra's wet. I unhook it then I unfasten the slide from my hair and begin to comb it out.

'Start at the ends,' that's what Gran always says. 'Be gentle, Helen, so that you do not make the hair to break.' She gave me a proper comb once. It had a silver back and wide, tortoiseshell teeth and it was hers when she was a girl. It had been one of the very few things that she found in a drawer upstairs, after the war, when she was released from the camp and finally went back home. She had put it in her pocket, she told me, together with a small green china dish. Then she'd closed the door on the family house that was empty now and she'd walked away down the street.

I open my wardrobe door and look at myself. It's an old-fashioned wooden wardrobe with a full-length mirror inside and lots of little drawers and shelves. It's the only thing in my room that's truly mine because I bought it. I paid five pounds at one of the Rook's jumble sales then Pat's father brought it round in his old camper van. My room was too small in that house so it stayed in the garage until we came here. I polished it last week but I haven't sorted it out yet. I just piled everything in. The mirror needs a good clean. I rub it with one of my T-shirts and then look at myself again as I slowly comb my hair.

'Helen? Dad says – oooh!' Luke stops in the doorway and claps his hand over his mouth. 'You *rude* thing! I can see your bottom! Yuk!' He wrinkles up his face. I turn round slowly so that he can see me. 'Aren't they big,' he giggles, between his fingers.

'Are they?'

'Oh yes. Much bigger than Mrs Edward's bosoms. She's only got little ones because Chris Owens saw them when we were swimming. And they smell, when she leans over.'

'It's her armpits that smell, you twit. Anyway, somebody should tell her to have a bath.'

'Should they?'

'Yes. But don't *you*. Anyway, who's Chris?'

'Just someone. But you don't smell, Helen.'

'Good. Now what does Dad want?'

He furrows his brow and hops from foot to foot.

'Is it about tea?'

'Yes! Tea's ready. That's it. That's what Dad said, and are you hungry because he's making toast?'

'Tell him I'll be down in a moment. And I'd love some toast.'

'OK.' He turns to go, then shoots back. 'Shall I tell him I've seen your . . . your thing as well?'

He slams the door and dashes off before I can reply. I stand there staring at myself. In the mirror, I can see the reflection of the refinery over my shoulder. There are a couple of flames but they're nothing special today and clouds are moving across fast. The wind is gusting the rain against my window so that everything in the glass dissolves and runs.

I ought to go downstairs, but before I do, I step closer, once again. I half close my eyes and tilt back my head. I look secretly down the slope of my cheek. That's what I'd look like, if I were asleep. If it was evening, or even night, and someone else was watching me, that's what they'd see.

There was a picture of the goddess Aphrodite in Tom's book. She was half-kneeling and the light shone on her marble breasts and the curve of her thighs. She was holding back her hair as though someone had just spoken to her and she had looked up. I remember it well. One day Tom had told me that I would look like that when I grew up, but I'd laughed and giggled and run away, because that was only a statue, and made of stone.

'Helen?' Dad shouts up the stairs.

'Coming!' I begin to dress. Outside, in the strengthening wind, the garden gate on to the cliff path begins to bang to and fro.

Chapter 10

'I suppose I *could* go.' Downstairs Dad chews his piece of toast. The rain has driven against the patio doors with such force that a pool of water has collected underneath. Dad stares at it, adjusts his glasses, then looks at me.

'Do *you* think I should go and fetch her, Helen?'

'Yes! Of course you should go!' Gran butts in. She's been nagging him to fetch Mum from the garden centre for the last ten minutes. 'Do you think it possible, Charles, to ride a bicycle in this weather? If you do, fine! But I'm telling you it is not! She will be blown off. Juliet will be blown into a ditch, a hedge . . . anything is possible. You've forgotten, Charles, what a storm can be like down here!'

'All right. Don't keep on.' Dad frowns.

'I'm not "keeping on". I'm only saying, only reminding you, because while you have been away in the South, you have forgotten things about this place. But I won't say it. Not if you don't want me to.' Gran pops in her last crust. She hasn't given up. She may have had her fill of hot buttered toast, but of conflict? Never!

'Will it be like a wreck?' Luke asks. 'When Mum's blown into a ditch by the storm? Mrs Edwards said that lots of ships are blown on to rocks and wrecked. Will Mum be?'

'No!' It's my turn to interrupt. 'There won't be anything like that. Mum'll be fine. She'll be back in a minute.'

'We hope,' Gran adds. 'That is what we always hope, isn't it? "They'll be back in a minute".'

'Mother –' Dad warns her, but she never takes any notice of him.

'Who'll be back in a minute?' Luke looks from one to another of us. His mouth is open and he's forgotten to chew. He doesn't follow what is going on. I'm not sure that I do, either.

I don't understand why Dad doesn't get up from his chair, start the car and go and look for Mum. It's a straight enough road from here to there. He can hardly miss her. It's not like him to try to stay in the warm. He'll do anything for anyone, too much so, Mum says. He's not the man for grand gestures but he'll always lend a hand. Hot buttered toast on a wet afternoon is his sort of thing exactly, not tea at the Ritz. When I was younger I wanted a more exciting father. I'd compare mine with Pat's dad. Rooky was brilliant, eccentric and exciting and colourful. My father, who used to be an accountant, could never be like that.

Pat said I was lucky with my father and now I agree. Like I said, he'll do anything for anyone. So I don't understand why he doesn't go and look for Mum.

Outside the rain is tipping down. The sky has darkened and the wind is dashing the last roses to bits. Petals and scattered autumn leaves are stuck to the patio like dabs of paint. We sit in silence, watching the rain. Then Dad suddenly lifts his head.

'That's her!' He jumps up.

I haven't heard anything but he's right. That's her voice and she's laughing as she puts her key in the door. She's still laughing in the hall and she's not alone.

'Oops,' her voice is loud. 'Mind that jug. That belongs to my mother-in-law. We don't want to knock that off!'

A man replies.

'Mum?' Luke runs to the door, then comes back. I don't move. I don't even look up.

'No,' I hear him say. 'I won't come in. I ought to get back.'

'Oh go on,' Mum's insisting. 'Come in and say hello to them all. I've got to change, but –'

'Juliet?' Dad gets up.

She pops her wet head in. 'Give me a moment, Charles. I'm drenched through. Look!' Her cheeks are pink and shiny with rain. Her T-shirt and jeans are sodden. She twirls round in the doorway with arms above her head and her small, bare feet are wet on the carpet. She's as excited as a kid, as though the storm is a huge joke and she's loving it. Maybe Dad guessed. Maybe that's why he didn't go and fetch her.

Before we can answer she bends down and kisses Luke on both cheeks then hurries upstairs. A moment later the shower is running. Luke wipes the drips from his cheeks and sidles over to my chair.

'It's *him*!' He whispers, digging his chin into my shoulder.

'I *know*,' I whisper back.

'Who? Who is it, then?' Gran hasn't recognized the voice.

'It's me, Mrs Kopperberg. It's Christian Owens.' He steps into the room, his red sweater darkened with rain. Gran is lost for words. 'I used to live just along from you, Mrs Kopperberg, in the old house. Don't you remember?' He smiles at her, then at Dad. 'Nice to see you both again. Juliet told me you were back and we, I've, been meaning to come over and say hello, since we're neighbours again. Well almost. But I expect you've heard about what's happened to Dad, so it's not been easy. But it's nice to see you again, Mrs Kopperberg. To see you all.' He smiles again and pushes back his wet hair. 'I'm sorry that I can't stop. I only brought Juliet back, because of the weather. I've put her bike by the garage for now. If that's all right?'

'That's very decent of you, Christian. Thanks a lot.' Dad stands up. 'I was just coming out myself, only you got in first. And just in time, by the look of her.'

'That's all right,' Christian nods at the rain. 'It's not a day to be out in, is it?'

'How's your mother?' Gran asks suddenly.

'My mother?' Christian rests his hands on the white cloth. 'Fine thanks, Mrs Kopperberg. I mean, as well as can be expected. Considering.'

Upstairs a door opens, then closes.

'Well, thanks again,' Dad moves towards the hall.

'That's all right. It was a pleasure.' Then he's gone.

'Well!' Gran begins almost before Dad has shut the front door. 'Well! What do you think of that?' she demands.

'Nothing! Nothing at all.' Dad's voice is unusually sharp.

Mum comes in wearing clean, dry clothes and with her hair slicked flat. She looks small and young.

'Has he gone already?' she asks.

'Yes!' Dad rubs his hands together. 'And thank goodness he has!'

'What do you mean?' Mum folds her arms.

'I mean I'm glad he's gone!'

'Thanks! Thanks a lot!' Mum picks up the teapot. 'And you didn't even offer him a cup of tea.'

'Why should I?' Dad shouts.

'Because,' Mum yells back, 'the guy gave me a lift home, for crying out loud! Which nobody around *here* seemed bothered about. What was I supposed to do, Charles? Say no?'

'Of course not,' Dad frowns.

'Yes!' Gran hisses. 'That's what you were supposed to

80

do, Juliet. You should have said no. Fancy bringing a man like that into this house!'

'But why, Anna? Just tell me why?' Mum has got control of herself again.

'I can't. Not now. Not in front of your children.'

'OK, I'll send them to their rooms. Then you can tell me. Luke! Helen!'

'No way!' It's my turn to shout. 'No way! I'm not being sent to my room like some *kid*. What are you all so worked up about, anyway? You should hear yourselves!'

'It's nothing,' Dad says, 'nothing at all.'

'It isn't "nothing", so stop pretending it is!' This time I yell.

'Helen, it's just –' Dad begins, but Luke makes a small, odd noise. He opens his mouth and vomits a sodden pile of sicked up tea and half-chewed toast on to the edge of the white tablecloth.

Gran scowls at me.

'Now look what you've done, Helen! Fancy frightening your little brother like that!'

'Me? What have *I* done?'

They don't answer because Luke has started to be sick again, this time on the floor.

We barely speak in the evening. Mum sits with Luke. She says he has a chill and must have caught it walking home in the rain. I shrug and go up to my room. I do tonight's homework and then some that doesn't have to be handed in until next week. Outside it's still pouring. The rain is so heavy that it's even blotted out the chimneys on the other shore. Out to sea a foghorn has begun to sound and it keeps on and on and on.

There's no point in going to bed yet. I'm too restless and anyway that noise won't let me sleep. I wish I had a decent pair of shoes for tomorrow because I don't want to get soaked. Even trainers would do. I should have made more of a fuss about losing my new ones, but it's difficult, when you're new. Then I remember Tom's.

Why shouldn't I? Anyway, they're not so strict about uniform in this school from what I've seen. And it's a shame not to use them, isn't it?

I wait until the house is quiet then I slip back down to the garage again.

'Mum!'

'Helen!' She has come in suddenly, in her dressing gown and wheeling her bike, while I have the box in my hands. We've made each other jump.

'I told you not to open those boxes, Helen.' She leans the bike in its place. 'I *asked* you not to.'

'I know Mum, but –'

'But *nothing*! Just shut them up again. Please?'

'No.'

'Please, Helen, just shut them up.'

'No!' I reach in and pull out one of his trainers. Then the other.

'Helen?' She's walking towards me over the concrete floor. Her hands are taut and outstretched as though she will snatch the trainers back. Or slap me.

She doesn't, though. She stops and stares at them and me. She folds her arms around herself, tucking her hands away inside her sleeves and shivering. It is cold down here, cold and dreary and it stinks of garage stuff: old, labelless tins of this and that and brushes encrusted with paint. There are green plastic petrol cans and car tyres and the dark red mud that has run in under the door. There's so much clutter left behind that Dad hasn't put the car in yet.

Mum shakes her head slowly as if she doesn't understand something. She doesn't speak.

I remember his shoes beside mine on the kerb. I liked to measure our respective sizes and I imagined that one day I'd catch him up. I'd press my leg against his but I'd shuffle forward secretly. I'd work my heel away, bringing our toes closer together. I'd think I'd tricked him and that he hadn't noticed.

'Not bad,' he'd say and I'd be so pleased. How dumb can you be? What girl in her right mind would want to take size nines? I'm only just getting used to it now and it's taken a lot of hard work. 'So what if you're *big*,' Pat always said. 'That's *you*.' But she was small and slim. "Anyway, I *like* you big, so there!" And that was Pat.

But when Tom and I had measured feet, I never thought ahead. I looked at the gap between his toes and mine and I grinned up at him, and he always smiled back.

'Watch!' I cried as I stepped off the kerb. I wanted to take one great big step. 'Watch me, Tom,' I shouted, half shutting my eyes with the thrill of it and the dazzling autumn sun that was low and bright.

'Helen?' Mum touches my arm. 'What is it, Helen?'

'Nothing. Nothing at all. You're right, Mum. I shouldn't have opened the box. I'll put them back.'

'No!' Mum continues to shake her head. 'No, *you're* right, Helen. You're *not* a kid and I shouldn't be telling you what to do. I'm sorry. Take them. Do *whatever* you like with them. It's just that I don't want to. Not anymore.'

'What don't you want to do?'

'Remember him. Not any more.'

'Mum!' I'm so shocked I don't know what to say.

Back in my room I kneel up, resting my forehead against the glass. Outside the marker buoys are flashing red in the wet black night. There's a sequence which Dad knows but I've forgotten. As I stare at them, I'm reminded of something red-eyed and awake. The flames beyond are pale as they weave and duck. The wind is so strong that I can imagine a piece of fire, a great torn sheet of flame being ripped off and wheeling through the sky like a chariot beyond control. Winged horses would snort and plunge. The steam from their flanks would scald and as their hooves struck the slate-sharp edges of the storm clouds, lightning would whiten the quiet hills and echo against the tipped red cliffs.

How could Mum say that?

I go back down and dial Pat's number.

'Pat?'

'It isn't Pat, it's Rooky here . . .' he's yawning. His voice is old and thick with sleep.

'I want Pat.'

'I think she's asleep now. That's Helen, isn't it?' He yawns again, then coughs himself awake. 'Helen? How are you?'

'It's just that . . .'

'Yes?'

'I opened the box. His box.'

'Yes? Wait a sec, I think Pat's almost here.' He's shouting for her to hurry up.

But I can't wait. Not any longer.

'I've found his shoes, his trainers, that he was wearing, that they've kept and wouldn't throw away, and . . .'

'And *what*? What is it Helen?'

'Nothing. I'm sorry, Rooky. I think I've made a mistake.'

'I tell you what,' he's speaking as if he and I have our elbows on the newspapers again. 'Isn't it half-term soon? How about a trip back? I've missed you, Helen. And even if Pat's too busy to see you, I'm not. How about it, Helen?'

It's nice of him and just what I'd expect but I'm not interested.

'Helen?' At last it's Pat and though she begs me to talk, I can't.

Softly, I lay the receiver down, so that she can't call back. Then I ease the telephone connection from its socket on the wall. Upstairs the trainers are side by side on the floor. Half shutting my eyes, I slip my feet in and stand up. They fit perfectly now, as if they were really mine.

Chapter 11

'Helen!' As I push open the fish shop door, Samantha Owens looks up from the chopping block. She's gripping a silver blue mackerel and a long-bladed knife is in her other hand. Her fingers are bloated and her knuckles purple. I didn't recognize her before she spoke. Her hair is hidden under a soiled cap. A white apron is tied around her stomach and she's even wearing white wellington boots. She looks older, like a woman at work.

'Wait a sec, Helen, and I'll be with you.' She slices off the head. The old lady waiting in front of me leans over to watch. Sam slits the belly, then tumbles the glistening guts into a bucket on the floor.

'Fresh, are they?' asks the old lady. 'Because he'll complain, otherwise. Men do, don't they? Won't get up from his chair to get it hisself, but not slow to complain. Soon as I'm back he'll come and watch me unwrap them and he'll ask if the fish are fresh. Silly old devil, that's all he's interested in now, his bit of tea. So *are* they fresh, love?'

Samantha dips her hand amongst the cut off fins and dead round eyes. She picks something out and I step back.

'Fresh is it, love?' the woman asks again.

Sam doesn't fling anything. She holds up a fish head, sticks a finger into its open mouth and waggles it in and out.

'See that, Mrs Lloyd? See these teeth? They're as sharp as razors, they are, and he's so fresh and frisky he could still bite my finger off if I let him go!'

'Get away with you, you little minx,' the old lady titters

as she gets a purse from her shopping bag. 'You're having me on. Aren't you?'

Sam winks after the woman has gone. She turns the fish head round.

'Here, that's what you look at, Helen. You look at the gills, where it breathes. See? They're bright red when you take a fish from the sea. Well, they would be, wouldn't they? Being full of blood.' She stares at the cut flesh for a moment, and at the pale, creamy core of the vertebrae. Then she laughs. 'These old girls all know that, because they've grown up round the dock, haven't they, but it makes them laugh every time. Some of them laugh so much they wet themselves. But it's like that with fish, isn't it?' She glances along the counter. Crabs and crayfish crouch on white plastic trays with their claws bound by tape and their absurd, stalked eyes stuck and still. There are cockles and scallops with some opened up, like bright orange kidneys. There are dishes of plaice with their frilled grey edges hanging over and between the pink shrimps and yellow slabs of smoked haddock there is a small tub of treacle-black laver bread. Gran likes it a lot but I'm not keen. At the back, a long, leathery eel is stretched out on a bed of crushed, blood-stained ice.

'Silly buggers, the lot of them!' Sam wrinkles up her nose. 'You wouldn't catch me swimming into no trawl net, not however fine its mesh, nor taking stuff from hooks either. Not now.'

I've never thought about fish like that. They had seemed quick and clever as they lurked in the crevices of rock pools, or flashed across as Tom and I leant over; rash maybe, and unlucky, definitely, when they twitched to and fro in the bucket, but not dumb. At the end of each day, I had been happy to crouch in the shallows and tip them back. I was glad when they swished their tails, raising a flurry of sand, and swam free.

'You come in for something, then?' Sam asks.

'Yes. Dad wants mackerel too. Or anything nice.' He had actually said 'fresh', but I'm not going to repeat that.

'How many?'

'Five. Or six, depending.'

'I'll look out the back for you, Helen. There's some come in this morning. Now they *are* fresh.'

She dries her hands across her stomach and stamps off across the spattered floor. It's cold in the shop despite the cheery posters on the wall.

'How about these, then?' They are stiff and bright and one seems to quiver as Sam tosses them down. She picks up the knife and sinks it into the skin. I hear it go through bone and a spatter of blood stains her cuff.

'Have you worked here long?'

She nods.

'Is it . . . fun?'

'Fun?' Sam looks up at the cracked white tiles and the sea-green walls. They are decorated with pictures of fish wearing aprons and straw hats and with platters of sea-food balanced on their fins. There's a stand of recipe cards in Welsh and English, and in a corner a plastic lobster is clipped on to a bit of plastic seaweed. 'Fun?' she repeats. 'Well, it's more fun than being dead, isn't it?' She laughs smokily as she drops my fish into a bag, then she jerks a printed carrier from the hook behind.

'It's my dad's shop. That's why I work, but it's not fun, even though fish are slippery buggers!' She laughs again. 'Tell you what, I'm off now for lunch, or could be. You like a coffee, then, Helen? We could walk up into town, couldn't we, if it's not raining too much. My treat.'

The dockside is crowded. She explains that several fishing boats have come in to shelter from the storm. A tall man in orange dungarees is adjusting a sodden tail of rope around a bollard on the quay. He looks up at Sam. He raises an eyebrow in some unspoken query but she shakes her head. Then he looks at me.

'This is my friend, Helen,' Sam says. 'Helen's in Wiffy's class in school. She's new around here, from – where you from, Helen?' Another slow glance has passed between the two of them.

'Surrey, outside London.'

'That so? London, eh? Like it here then, do you, in sunny Pembrokeshire?' The man hooks black thumbs through the buckles of his dungarees and flexes his legs.

'Yes I do. It's very nice here.'

'It can be.' He glances up at the storm clouds. 'When the sun's out, that is. Can't it, Sam? It can be nice, can't it, on a boat? Though I'm surprised your Christian's going out again.' He turns slowly and shields his eyes. 'The forecast said there was more weather coming in. A lot more, it said.'

Then I see what he's looking at: the *Black Pig* has left a mooring, and is moving between the rows of boats. The engine gives out a cloud of smoke and a ripple of water breaks on the bow. Christian is at the helm.

'We've got to eat, haven't we?' Sam mutters. The man narrows his eyes as Christian turns the wheel and brings the boat round into the lock.

'That's what it is, is it? And I thought a good son like that would be out looking for his old dad.' Sam doesn't say a thing and I suddenly remember what Christian had said on top of the cliff.

'Be seeing you sometime, shall we, Sam?' Their eyes meet again.

'I dunno.' She pushes back her hair. 'I'm pretty busy now. What with school.'

'School!' he laughs. 'You?'

'Why not?' She grabs my arm, pushing hers through and she holds on tight. 'That's what we're doing right now. It's school stuff, isn't it, Helen?'

'Yes. We're going to the library. For school.'

'Well,' he mocks, 'don't let me stop you. It's a wonderful thing, education.' He's climbing back on board. 'Or so they tell me! Eh, Helen?'

I don't know what to say. Sam pulls my arm. I want to go too but the man is clambering along the deck, keeping pace with us.

'What do *you* think about education, then? Helen?' He calls my name in a lingering way. I shouldn't look round but I do. I want to watch the *Black Pig* and Christian but I catch the man's eye instead. He's leaning over the side of the boat. 'Helen,' he repeats, as our eyes meet. 'Lovely name you've got.' Suddenly, he's directly beneath me and looking up. I step away from the edge and he laughs, sucking air between his teeth which are big and widely spaced. 'Helen? Weren't that some goddess like, or some queen?' He bites his bottom lip. His eyes fix on mine, then drop. 'That surprised you, didn't it? Eh, Miss Troy? I can see it did. You didn't think I'd know about that, but I do. I know a lot of things. And so does she.' He jerks his head at Sam, then re-examines me.

'I'm not stupid and I know a trick or two, even though I haven't been to school. Eh, Sam?' Then he begins to sing:

A little boat sails on the alley alley oh,
the alley alley oh, the alley alley oh,
a little boat sails on the alley alley oh
*on the last day of September**

*Anon, *Faber Book of Colloquial Verse*.

90

'Piss off, Glyn!' Sam pushes in front of me. 'Piss off, you filthy –'

He roars with laughter and lets something fall down so suddenly that it makes us both jump.

'Goodbye then, Helen of Troy!' He shouts again.

'Dirty bugger,' Sam scowls as she puts the tray down on the café table. 'I hope you like chips, Helen, because I do, with mayonnaise.' She dips one in and bites it off. 'Or with blue cheese dressing, that's my favourite, but they don't have it here.'

'Who was he?' I ask.

'My Uncle Glyn. That's who.'

'Your mother's brother?'

'No, no. My dad's.' She takes another chip and messes with the mayonnaise. 'You know what happened to my dad?'

'Not really.'

'Nor do I.' Then she fumbles for her fags. 'You don't mind, do you? It's why I come in here, even though they don't have the blue cheese. But I won't offer you one.' She hunches over and clicks at the lighter. 'Because smoking's no good, is it? It'll kill me, that's what everybody says, and I believe them. I really do. Only I don't care. But don't you start, Helen. Not if you haven't already. It's a filthy habit. See that?' She bunches up a handful of her hair and sniffs. 'Even I can smell the smoke, smell my own stink! Still,' her laughter crumbles through her cough, 'maybe it's better than fish, because those slimy blighters get everywhere and not just on your hands. But go on, Helen, eat up. You haven't had your share.'

I try. She watches me and lights another fag.

'You don't want to take no notice of my uncle. He didn't mean nothing. He's just a fool,' she shrugs.

'It's OK. I know what you mean.'

91

'That book,' she says unexpectedly, 'that book you lent our Wiff.'

'Yes?'

'He likes it a lot you know and won't let anyone else have a look at it. But I did. I didn't bother to read it because I didn't want to but I looked at those pictures of these great big blokes with no clothes on, and those animals, especially that spotted one. Black and spotted he was, with a bull's head and a tail.'

'The Minotaur?'

'I don't know the name. Like I said, I didn't have time to read. I just looked, and then I put it back, so he wouldn't know.'

'It wasn't just for Wiffy, it was for all of you.'

'I know. *I* understand that, but not Wiffy. He thinks it's special for him and he can get mad, you know, very mad indeed if someone touches his stuff. So I put it back. You won't say, will you?' She takes another chip. 'He can't help it, you know. Not really.' She looks at me quickly. 'He's not like your brother.'

'Like *Luke*?'

'No! Not Luke!'

'You mean . . . Tom?'

She nods.

'But you never knew Tom. Apart from that day on the beach.'

'Didn't I?'

I picture her again: her thin legs as she paddled at the water's edge and her black hair, tangled up and knotted with the sand and wind and salt. I remember how she'd screwed up her eyes against the sun and I remember what she'd said.

'You called him a coward.'

'I know,' she looks away. 'And I'm sorry about that.'

92

She's scratching at the nicotine-stained lump on her fore-finger. 'I shouldn't have done that, should I? I was really ashamed after. Especially when I saw what he did for you.'

'What do you mean? What did he do?'

'Well, you'd have drowned, wouldn't you, Helen? Or had your skull smashed in. That's what Christian said after-wards, because the tide was well on the turn and there's a strong undertow in that bay. That's why no one ever swims there, or no one local. And especially when the tide's on the turn and the water's rushing back. Your brother must have known that when he dived, mustn't he, because they say you can see the currents even more clearly from where he was, see the water rushing out and the rocks underneath. But he still dived, didn't he? For *you*?'

Then I realize that I never saw Tom dive, never really knew what he'd done until I felt his arm under my chin. But she had.

'I've never seen anyone do that,' she murmurs.

'Do what? The Red Rock Dive?'

'Not *just* that. What I mean is, I've never seen anyone risk themselves like that, for someone else. My family wouldn't do it, would they? Not for me.'

'Of course they would! Why ever not? If someone fell into the sea, *you'd* help.'

'Would I?' she asks.

'Yes, of course!'

'I didn't.' She pulls her hair over her face and then I remember what happened on the rocks.

'It was an accident.'

'Was it?' she asks.

'Yes! And we were only kids.'

'Kids!' she snorts, then is silent, smoking her fag. 'Were we? Were we ever that?'

'Yes, of course we were! It was *kid's* stuff, and ages ago.'

'The thing is,' she coughs and clears her throat, 'he was my hero. He was my pin-up, after that.'

'Who was?'

'Tom. Who else? Other kids had pop stars in their pencil boxes and on their walls but I didn't. I had Tom. He was all I ever wanted.'

'What do you mean?' I don't believe her and I don't want to hear any more. I just want to crawl away and hide myself and my monstrous jealousy. I don't want anyone to ever see the gaping wound she's made.

'I liked your brother, Helen. I liked him a lot.' She pushes back her hair.

'You were only a little girl!' I hear my voice as mean and suspicious as Gran's. Sam has cut through my skin and I can't bear it. 'You were my age!' I protest.

'So? Who says you can't fall in love then? Anyway, I wasn't your age, was I? I was older than you, even then. Eleven I was, that year, and almost twelve.'

'But you can't have been! Not if you're in the year above?'

'Why not?' Her tone is defiant. 'Why can't I be older? Because I *am*. But I'm stupid, see? I'm so stupid I had to stay down in school. That's what teachers do to kids who don't learn. They say they're stupid. So it's not just our Wiffy, is it? It's me, too! In fact it's the whole Owens family. We're too stupid to know about your Minotaurs. In fact we're all too stupid to know anything!'

Chapter 12

'Did you get the fish?' Dad asks as I push open the gate. He's perched on the ladder, hacking at the hedge.

'Yes.' I hold up the bag.

'Good. But what about the shoes? Couldn't you find anything you liked?' Dad's tactful. He'd never say 'anything big enough', because he understands how I feel about my feet.

'Not really.' I don't tell him that I didn't look. He needn't know that all I had wanted to do was get away from Samantha, and come home.

' "Owens Fish",' he reads the jingle from the bag. ' "Hat's off to Owens Fish, Toppers in any dish".' He grimaces. 'That can't be *David* Owens' shop, can it?'

I shrug.

'But it could be, couldn't it?' he muses. 'That awful bit of verse reminds me of old pirate Jack, the grandfather. He liked a bit of poetry and he made up bad verse too. It was the most dreadful doggerel. And the drunker he was, the worse the verse, but he was always spouting it. So I can imagine David going in for the same sort of rubbish, though I can't think how he got the money together to buy a shop. Still, as long as we stay clear of them.' He begins to climb down the ladder. 'Who was in the shop? Not his wife, surely?'

'No, she wasn't. But why does it matter anyway? I thought you wanted to keep clear of them.'

'I do, and there's no reason. I was just thinking.'

'Thinking what?'

He doesn't answer, but lops off a bit more. He's really

had a go at the hedge and it looks a mess.

'I wanted a better view,' he says, climbing down, to stand beside me. 'I couldn't see anything from my office. Not with that hedge there. Do you think I've overdone it?' He's fiddling with the secateurs, snapping them to and fro. 'Still, I dare say it'll grow back.' He shrugs. 'Look here, would you like to go somewhere else, Helen, to get these shoes? We could go now.' He looks at his watch. 'There's still time.'

'Not really, Dad.'

'Oh well.' He's disappointed. 'There are more storms forecast and we can't have you going around with wet feet, can we?'

I want to accept his offer. It would be nice to go out. We'd both enjoy it and I do need those shoes. He'd buy me a replacement sports bag and trainers, if I mention it, but I don't. I don't want him to be nice to me.

'Why *did* you ask about Mrs Owens?'

'I don't know, Helen!' He kicks the pile of clippings he's left by the gate.

'Yes, you do. You and Gran are always hinting unpleasant things about the Owens, so what's wrong with them? Do you think they sell poisoned fish!'

'Yes. Highly likely!'

'Dad!'

'I know, I know. I shouldn't have said that. So what did you buy from them? Mackerel?'

'Yes. Sam said they were the freshest. She got them from the back specially.'

'I'm sure they'll be fine.' He reclimbs the ladder and savages a bit more. Somewhere, further round the coast path, someone must be having a bonfire. The smoke reminds me of autumn in our old garden and old leaves and clearing up.

'Who's Sam?' he asks suddenly.

'Samantha Owens. She's the daughter and in the year above me at school.'

'Look, Helen. Do let's go and get you some decent shoes. *I'd* like to. I'm sick of this hedge.'

'Not today, Dad. I've got this geography project. It's about the coast.'

'Fine.' He turns his back on me and burrows into the hedge as if he doesn't want to hear any more. As I walk towards the house I hear him hacking through.

The kitchen smells of fruit cake which is a pleasant surprise. It's one of my favourites and ages since Gran made one.

'Who's coming to tea?'

'No one!' It isn't Gran who's taking the cake out of the oven, it's Mum. She's wearing an apron over new jeans. Flour smears an eyebrow but she looks pleased with herself. 'Close the door, Helen. Quick. Cold air might make it sink.' Luke is perched on a stool scraping out the mixing bowl.

'Feeling better?' I ask him.

'No.' He wipes off another fingerful and sucks.

'I thought a cake would cheer him up,' Mum jiggles it loose from its tin.

'Not *fruit* cake!' Luke protests. 'I told you. I don't *like* fruit cake.'

'Yes you do! I haven't made one for so long, you've forgotten. Look how you're enjoying that.'

'I *don't* like fruit cake!' he whines. 'I told you, Mum. And this isn't cake, it's just mixed up things, and it isn't cooked!' He pushes the bowl from him and scowls. 'I wanted chocolate! I told you I only like chocolate now!' He jumps down and stamps out of the kitchen. Mum's face falls.

'What's up with him?' I ask.

'He didn't sleep well.' Mum frowns as she peels the

97

greaseproof paper off. 'I thought he'd enjoy helping me. But maybe he isn't up to it. He's not well.'

'Rubbish. He's just spoilt.'

'Helen!' She spins round.

'He *is*, Mum, honestly, he's turning into a spoilt brat. "I only like chocolate," ' I mimic.

She doesn't reply, just fusses with the cake which sits and steams on the rack. Still, it's ages since she's made anything as nice as this and I should be pleased.

'What's this?' Gran comes in too.

'Cake! What do you think it is?' I didn't mean to snap.

'Helen!' Mum protests again.

'You'd better give me those fish,' Gran holds out her hand, 'your bad temper will make them go off.'

'I'm not bad tempered. I'm just telling the truth.' I look at Mum. I want her to help me out, but she won't. She's obsessed with her stupid cake and can't stop staring at it.

'I just said that Luke was spoilt, Gran, that's all. I mean, look at his shoes. His *new* shoes. He wrecked them last week and if I hadn't cleaned them up they'd be in a terrible state.'

'*You* cleaned his shoes last week?' Gran frowns. 'So it was *you*, who marked the cloth?'

I can't believe I'm hearing this.

'That's right,' I look Gran in the eye. 'Go on. Blame me!'

'Helen!' But that's all Mum says.

'You *always* blame me!' I mutter. It's true and I'm used to it, so I don't know why I'm making such a fuss this time. But my heart's thumping unpleasantly.

'Go on with you,' Gran is scornful. 'Don't be so silly. Of course I don't blame you! Now, Juliet, shall I put that on a plate for you?'

'It needs to cool down,' Mum doesn't look at me. 'And it's not for today.'

'Not for today?' Gran asks.

They've forgotten me already and are totally preoccupied with that cake. You'd think nobody had ever made one before. I find Luke halfway up the stairs, sitting in a patch of sunlight. Suddenly he doesn't look spoiled. He's pale and his eyes are dark-ringed, and I'm ashamed of what I said.

'It's the little black bits,' he sniffs. 'That's what I hate.'

'Do you mean the raisins and currants? But they're only grapes, dried. And you used to like those didn't you?' I sit down too and put my arm round him.

'Yes, but not *burnt*. That's what I *hate*, when they're all black and burnt and they crunch in your mouth. She wouldn't listen to me, Helen. It's like eating burnt mud.'

'Is it?' I remember the foods I hated. It wasn't only beetroot, it was steak too, with its threads of flesh which jammed in my teeth and made my jaws ache. And peppermint. Years ago Tom and I had made peppermint creams and I'd scoffed my entire share even though they were for Christmas presents. Afterwards I couldn't bear the taste of peppermint, or even the smell.

'But when do you eat mud?'

'When –' He takes off his specs.

'When what?'

'Football,' he mutters, 'that's when.'

'I thought you liked football.'

'I do!' He jumps up.

'But not the mud?'

He shakes his head.

'Anyway, Mum said I haven't got to eat it.'

'Eat what?'

'The fruit cake. Mum said she'd buy chocolate. She promised. She said I could have as much chocolate as I like when he comes. So I won't be left out. She promised, Helen.'

'When *who* comes?'

'That man.' He frowns.

'What man?'

'That tall man who brought her back in the rain, the one she's always talking about. The one who's going to be a new brother. That's why she's made the cake. It's for him, because his Mum doesn't, and he's coming to tea tomorrow. But she hasn't got the chocolate yet.'

'When does she talk about him?' I ask.

'I don't know,' Luke shrugs. 'All the time.'

I can hear Dad in the kitchen. He's joking as he washes his hands. 'Wretched hedge is as tough as old boots so I think I've earned a big slice of that!'

'You can't,' Mum's voice is clear. 'I can't cut it yet, it'll crumble and fall apart.'

Dad's not listening. He's drying his hands on the roller-towel and whistling. Her cakes are delicious, he's saying, the best in the world, whether in slices or crumbs.

Poor, stupid Dad.

'Tough,' I shout, barging back in. 'Mum hasn't made it for *us*. She's made it for *him*.'

'What?' Dad's jaw drops. 'What are you talking about Helen?'

Mum turns away.

'Well?' I demand. 'Who's the cake for, Mum?'

'It's not definite,' she's speaking reluctantly. 'Not yet. But he said he'd try and come. If he could.'

'Who?' Gran asks sharply.

'Mum?' I prompt but I know what she's going to say.

'Well, Christian, actually. Young Christian Owens. I've asked him to tea.'

'What!' Dad and Gran explode.

'You can't!' I've never heard Dad say that before.

Mum bends over her cake, and brushes some crumbs into her hand.

'Well, Charles,' she licks a finger, dips it into her palm and tastes. 'I can, actually, and I am. I like Christian. We all do at the garden centre: so I've asked him to tea on Sunday. I know what you think about his family but I don't agree with you. I feel sorry for him, he's just a young guy. Fancy losing a father like that! He blames himself and now everyone round here is suggesting that he had something to do with it. It's outrageous.'

It's more than I expected, more than any of us did. Mum takes off her apron and folds it up.

'Juliet?' Dad pleads.

'No!' She shakes her head. 'I'm *not* talking about this, Charles. I'm doing it. And it will be nice to have a young man in the house again. I've missed that.'

They look at each other as if they are alone and we are not present at all.

'Well, Juliet,' Gran's old voice is clear. 'I am sure you have baked a nice cake but I shall not be here to enjoy my slice tomorrow. I have just remembered an old friend and I shall visit her tomorrow afternoon.'

'Can I come, too?' Luke interrupts. 'Will she have chocolate, Gran?'

'Oh no!' I mutter not quite under my breath. 'You'll miss tea with your nice new brother!'

'Helen!' Mum protests.

'But you needn't bother, Mum. Christian Owens won't be coming tomorrow because I've just seen him setting out to sea. So dream on, Mum! No feeding cake to your brand new son!'

In a moment I'm out of the door and on to the cliff path. Banks of cloud are building up again and darkening the sky.

101

A wind is blowing up the channel, touching the tops of the grey waves with breaking crowns of white. Above the flame stretches itself. It's pale today, as pale as straw or the winter sun on the edge of a hill. The wind combs through it, snagging and tearing bits off. Fragments of fire flicker in the sky but the flame reaches out like a greedy tongue and licks them back.

On the little beach at the foot of the cliffs, children are playing with a dog. They're throwing stones into the surf and urging it in. I stand and watch, letting the wind blow in my face.

'Helen!'

Even if one of them has come after me, I'm not going home, not yet. I turn towards them, but no one is there.

How could Mum do that to me? Tom never was *her* brother. He was only her son, so she doesn't know what it's been like. She has no idea.

'Helen!'

A brief, bright edge of sun seeps under the storm clouds and almost dazzles me. I stand quite still and, although no one is about, I can almost see him again.

He wore shirts in the summer, old blue shirts, with the sleeves rolled up over his golden forearms. The collars were frayed at the back and Gran used to grumble, but he didn't care and I liked to pick off the little threads. I'd lean close and tweak them out with my face buried in his warm hair. He had a mole on the back of his neck. I'd touch it sometimes and tickle him and he'd pull me over his shoulders into his arms. He'd tickle me round my ribs and call me his little bird. Sometimes he'd pretend to be a crocodile and he'd snap his jaws, and I'd be one of those little birds that hops around and picks bits out of crocodiles' teeth.

Tom was my brother. Mine alone and no one can take

that from me, or replace him, no matter how hard they try. Not Sam and definitely not Mum. They never knew the games we played on summer evenings, when the sun was low, and yet, like pickpockets, they want to sidle close to me and snatch it all away.

'Helen?'

But there's no one there, and now the clouds have blotted out the sun.

Chapter 13

'Helen!' Wiffy steps out from nowhere at all. 'I'm sorry! Helen, I didn't mean to frighten you. Don't be cross.'

I catch at the twiggy branches along the cliff path and cling on as the ground tips and the sky swings. I can't get a firm enough grip because it's not a tree, just a scrubby bush covered with brambles and old man's beard. It's rough and ragged on the cliff edge, and only just hanging on itself. I've scratched my hands and face but I haven't fainted. As the path slides back, I let the dark stems hold me up.

'Helen?' Wiffy Owens touches my arm. His face is chalk white. He's holding on to me too, his mouth open, his brown eyes sliding with fear, or terror. 'I didn't mean to frighten you. I'd never do that.'

I don't know which of us is more shocked. His breath is hot and sour on my neck. I can feel him against me, like some cringing pet wanting to be stroked.

'Helen?' His eyes are half closed, his head pressed against my breasts as though he expects to be hit.

'I'm sorry,' he breathes and his hand moves.

A large black dog runs up and sniffs and we leap apart.

'Look at Wiffy Owens! Hiyah, Wiff!' It's the children from the beach with their dog and sticks.

'What you doing then, Wiff?' They're sniggering, looking from him to me. I recognize one from my school. Another taller boy, with gap teeth, was in the playground last week with Luke. The dog runs to and fro and lifts a leg along the bushes. The tall boy wipes his sleeve over his nose.

'We seen you up there, Wiff Owens, we seen your smoke. It was you, wasn't it, on the cliff, what lit that fire?'

'It wasn't!'

'It *was*, because I seen you. I was on the beach and I was watching you. But you didn't see me. Too busy was you, Wiff? With her?' He grins boldly. The others howl with laughter and shove each other about. Wiffy runs at them.

'No!' he yells. 'No, I weren't. And I'll tell your dad what you said, you filthy little rat!' He charges them, arms flailing and feet flapping but he covers no ground. They scatter lazily, then regroup waving their sticks. They know he'll never catch them. A 'born again penguin', that's what Pat called kids like Wiff.

'Want to get me, do you, Wiffy? Want to give me one too? Come on then!' The gap-toothed boy clenches his fists and sways from side to side.

'Don't,' I put out my hand. 'They're only kids.'

'That's right, Wiffs. We're only kids. So be a good boy and do what Mummy says!' The tall one dances closer, waggling his hips. 'Because she's big enough, isn't she!'

'I'll kill you!' Wiffy screams. 'And I'll tell your dad!'

The children run but when they're far enough away, the smallest looks back.

'And I'll tell *yours*, Wiffy Owens,' he shrieks, 'I'll tell your dad what you done.'

'You can't, you nut,' the tall boy is scornful, 'Wiffy's dad's already dead!'

The gloom swallows them up and all I can hear is their running feet on the path and the scrape of the black dog's claws.

'I didn't do it,' Wiffy tilts his head back.

'Do what?'

'Nothing. Only I didn't, Helen, honestly, I didn't.'

'So what if you *did*? There's no law against lighting fires, is there?'

He stares at me.

'No,' he says, 'not against that.'

We walk slowly back past the gate in our fence and stop at the bend in the path where an old holly bush grows over.

'Come on,' Wiffy says. 'You can follow me, if you like.' He holds out a hand. I don't take it but the holly catches as I brush past and underfoot the debris of the summer rustles and slides: crisp packets and supermarket bags, and here and there a bottle and an empty can.

'Careful,' he says. 'Be careful here.' As my eyes adjust to the gloom I see a low wall that has crumbled away. He steps past and I follow and below us waves are breaking on the beach.

'Well?' he asks.

I can't see anything at all.

'What do you think, Helen?'

The flame on the opposite shore is flecked like the eye of something waiting to pounce.

'I could make it bigger, Helen. If you wanted. I could add another room. I've thought about it already.'

Then I realize that we are standing in a den built into the hedge on top of the cliff. It's a pretend house, a camp; it's kids' stuff, and Wiffy's secret place.

Years ago Tom made a den. It was behind the museum, where the shed and the fence formed a corner. He laid a flat stone floor. I can't remember where he'd got the slabs, but they were huge. I couldn't shift them at all, but he'd let me mix mud in an old paint tin instead of cement. We dropped in chopped up straw and clumps of my hair. He cut loads off one afternoon. I was pleased, and Gran was cross later because it hadn't grown back when we came down here for our holidays. We dropped in my hair and straw and other stuff, and I churned it round and round. He'd wanted eggs as well because the books said that was how builders made plaster in ancient times, but Mum wouldn't give him any, so we spat instead. We shot globules of spit on to the mud and I'd stirred and grumbled that it wasn't fair because his spit balls were bigger than mine. He built walls and there had even been a window. I wanted curtains, but he said 'no', though we had cushions on the red milk crates we used as seats.

'What d'you think?' Wiffy asks.

'It's lovely, Wiffy. It's really nice.' But there's nothing here at all, just a trampled space behind a holly bush. It's rubbish, just like his wreck.

I look around and smell the earthy damp of Tom's den again. We had stored sugar in a rusting mustard tin and he had screwed hooks into the fence post to hang things on, though they'd have used forked sticks in the olden days, he said. The door was a problem: rain and leaves blew in. He'd hung up a sack and though it always dripped and got wood lice, it had felt like a door. The den had felt like a house too, even though I could always see sky through the branches on its roof.

'Do you really like it, Helen?'

'Yes.' It's like being a child again even though I've grown up.

'And you can see the flame so well can't you, Helen?'

'Yes.'

'I can see whatever I want with a flame!' He is crouching by the remains of the fire. When he blows, the ash fans out and I can smell it in the air. Suddenly I see a spark, the tiny ruby heart of an ember and then the nimble, scrambling flame. He feeds it with gorse and holly so that it crackles and spits.

107

'What can you see, Wiffy?'

'Everything,' he grins. 'Especially at night. It shows me whatever I want.'

I don't know how to answer him, so I shrug and look away.

'I bet you've got tea in here,' I smile at last.

Tom and I made tea. We'd had a camping kettle and a battered, non-stick pan that Mum had chucked out. Occasionally we fried bacon, but Tom's speciality, which I loved best, was something made from flour and water and a pinch of salt. We wound the dough round sticks and cooked them over the open fire. Mine used to fall off and burn, but Tom always made more and gave me some of his.

'Course I've got tea. And milk,' Wiffy says. He pulls out an old garden chair and opens it up. 'You'd be surprised what folk throw out, Helen. I get all my stuff like that.' He puts on more twigs and when the fire's burning steadily he fills a kettle from a plastic bottle and balances it on bricks.

'You cold, Helen?'

'A little.'

He brings out a bit of rug and tucks it over my legs. The wind is driving the clouds across the evening sky, although we are protected here behind the wall. The fire burns steadily and I can feel its warmth touch my cheeks. Below us on the beach the incoming tide laps at the rocks.

'I did what it wrote in your book,' Wiffy says suddenly. He reaches across and picks a long stem of some plant from the shadows.

'See?' he blows through it, so that the flame flares. 'It's hollow.'

'What is it, Wiffy?'

'It's fennel! I bet you didn't know that!'

'What are you talking about Wiffy?'

He shifts closer and rests his arm on the chair.

'Your book what you gave me, Helen, it wrote things about Prometheus. It explained how he carried that stolen fire down from Mount Olympus without him being seen. It said that he broke an ember off the sun and stuck it in a "pithy stalk of fennel", which I thought was pretty good. That's how Prometheus carried fire down the mountain without Zeus seeing, so he could give it to the people at the bottom who didn't have no fire and must have been ever so cold. Like you, Helen, without no flame. I tried it myself but I burnt my hand. See?' He shows me several livid marks on his palm. Again, I don't know what to say.

'D'you think I'm stupid, Helen?'

I shake my head.

'But you didn't expect me to know things like that, did you? Or try them.'

'Well . . .'

'But I *do*.' He grins and tilts back his head. 'Nobody thinks I can read properly and it's easier that way, isn't it? When you don't know anything, folks can't ask.'

'Ask what?'

'Nothing!' he answers quickly. 'So you won't tell, will you, Helen?'

'No.'

'Because there's one who suspects.'

'Suspects?'

'Yes. It's that Mrs Cable. She watches what's going on and I don't want no one messing with me. Though someone did, the other day. Some bastard came in here and kicked this place to bits. But I think I know who did it, and I'll get them in the end.'

I shiver despite the rug.

' "Pithy",' he says suddenly. 'That's the one word I

didn't know. What's a *"pithy"* fennel stalk, Helen? Have you any idea?'

'It's like the pith you get round oranges, and grapefruits, it's that soft white flesh, under the skin.'

He leans close.

'Maybe the fennel that grew in Ancient Greece was more pithy,' I lean away as I try to explain. 'It's a hot country, so maybe those plants grew with more pith. Perhaps in those days people did put hot embers in fennel stalks and carry them that way, without the fire going out, or them burning their hands.'

'Maybe.' He's watching my mouth.

'My brother Tom would have known about that. He knew everything about the Greeks. He knew –

'More than me?' His voice is eager. As I nod, I feel his hand begin to move. In the darkness, I can see nothing but the flame.

'Helen?' Dad's voice breaks into the night. I hear our gate bang and his tread along the path.

A torch beam swings to and fro.

'Helen!' He calls again.

'Don't go,' Wiffy's hand is on my thigh, under the rug. 'Please, Helen. Don't go.'

'I *must*. It's my dad.' The torch beam moves along.

'Is that what you've got, Helen?' he breathes into my hair. 'Soft white flesh under your skin?'

'Wiffy!' I push him away so violently that he stumbles into the fire. I jump up, scramble past the holly bush and make my way back to the path.

Chapter 14

I catch Dad up at the garden gate. He's blundered into the pile of hedge cuttings in the dark so I hold his torch while he kicks himself free.

'Sorry, Dad, I didn't notice how far I'd gone.' I'm waiting for him to be annoyed but he isn't. We walk to the patio in silence and he doesn't even ask me where I've been. I'm cold. I want him to put his arm round me and nag.

'Helen,' he's staring at Mum in the lighted kitchen window, 'about that young man . . .'

'Yes?' Does he think that's where I've been? Meeting Christian along the cliff path, and in the dark? 'What about him, Dad?'

'There was trouble years ago, Helen, and I should have said. David Owens was in my class when we were kids. He used to come to school with bruises all over him. Everybody said it was the father, Jack. They said that he beat his wife and his sons too. When she sickened and died people gossiped that Jack was to blame, though no one ever knew. Anyway, that left him with two young lads and things went from bad to worse. David came to school less and less and the younger brother, Glyn, hardly at all. Old Jack was a drunk, not so bad when he was sober, but a hard man and it's a hard life at sea, or that's what people said.' Dad shakes his head; he's not a hard man.

'Nothing was done, and I think that was more the way then. Some people still thought Jack Owens was doing all right with those boys, who were wild, there's no doubt about that. Whenever there was a fight in town you could guarantee that one of the Owens was in the thick of it and sometimes both. Then David Owens did time inside. I don't know the details but your Gran does, because they were neighbours in the old house at the time. Anyway, the next thing we know is that he's brought this young girl home.'

'Sylvia?'

'Yes! But, how do you know her name?'

'I read it in the paper, Dad. There was an article about the *Black Pig*.'

'I see. Well, she was a pretty little thing, black-haired, slim, training to be a nurse, I think, and over from Ireland. Your Gran never understood what a girl like that could see in a man like David Owens but in no time there was a baby on the way, and she'd given up her nursing and she married him, just like that.'

'So?'

'So it started all over again, didn't it? Screams in the night and this young woman, Sylvia, you say her name is, running to neighbours, with him following behind, kicking down their doors, demanding her back. It was bedlam, your Gran said.'

I try to imagine Sylvia young and pretty, but all I can think about is Sam and Wiffy and Christian too, watching all this. It makes me feel cold and ill as if I've picked up Luke's chill. I don't want to hear any more.

'Then,' he continues, 'she left. Just got up one morning and walked to the station and got on the first train. She didn't even have the money for a ticket because a neighbour saw her in Cardiff, stopped at the barrier. She was sobbing, and trying to explain.'

'And she left the children behind? With a father like that?'

I remember the summer of the Red Rock Dive. Were they already alone?

'Oh yes. She couldn't have cared less. And that's when they started coming round, upsetting your Gran. The girl especially –'

'You mean *Sam*?

'That's right. At first she was always at the door, though your Gran never encouraged her. She said that that girl was trouble and I expect she still is. Is she?' He asks suddenly.

'I don't know.' I look away. I wanted to say 'yes'.

'I thought you said she was at school.'

'She *is* but I don't *know* her. I only bought that fish.'

'Good. I don't want you to know her, Helen, and I don't want her brother, that Christian Owens, in our house either.'

'Dad!' I'm shocked.

'OK. I know you disapprove. *I* disapprove! I'm a counsellor, for heaven's sake. I keep confidences and I certainly don't spread malicious gossip. But this is different, Helen. Look what's happened to the father: disappeared at sea and even the police must have their doubts. It's a mess, a real rat's nest and I don't want your mother involved. You know how vulnerable she is. That's why she doesn't do the charity work any more. She gets too upset.' He sighs bitterly. 'I should have said something when she first began talking about Christian Owens. I should have warned her off then.'

'When did she start talking about him?'

'I don't know. As soon as she began that job. It was "Christian this" and "Christian that". I don't want her involved.'

'Involved?'

'Why has she asked him *here*, Helen?'

'Dad! It's only *tea*! She's saying "thank you" because he brought her home. That's all it is!'

'Is it?' he asks.

'Yes!' I don't meet his eye, because I don't believe what I've said. I don't believe a single word of it but I want Dad to agree. I need him to smile, to say he's made a mistake and to laugh at himself for being a fool. Only he doesn't.

'Is that all this is?' he asks me, as we pause at the door to kick the mud from our feet.

'Yes! He's just a workmate. She's saying "thank you" because he brought her home. That's all it is.'

'Helen!' Gran runs to me as soon as I step inside. 'Thank goodness your father has found you and brought you home. I keep telling him that that is what he must do. But he waits, your father. He waits too long. And you, Helen, you must not go out into the night like that. It is not safe for a young girl, and on the cliff path too!'

'I'm sorry,' I put my arm round her because she's upset. 'You're right, I shouldn't have done that. I went further than I thought. I'm sorry about that.'

'It is because you are still young, Helen. You cannot know of all the bad things in the world. And should not. That is why you have your family. Is that not so, Juliet?'

Mum pulls a face and shrugs. She has been listening in silence and I know why. She hasn't been anxious about me at all. She couldn't care less. She's thinking about him, her 'new' son. This is her new start and it takes my breath away. Gran strokes back my hair but Mum doesn't say a word. Over at the sink, Dad runs some water and washes his hands.

And Sunday never ends. Mum has been waiting all day but Christian doesn't arrive. She wanders about, fiddling in the garden and reading to Luke but she avoids me. I don't care. I watch as she puts on new, tight jeans, then takes them off. Later she tries a skirt. I know what she is doing. Skirts are more motherly and the proper thing for a new,

114

grown-up son. Unfortunately Mum's skirt is too short. It looks pathetic and it shows the veins on her legs. I'm not going to mention it. I'm not saying a word.

I don't say anything at tea either. It's only the four of us and we eat our cake in silence. Even Luke must have understood that something is up because he silently nibbles the centre out of his slice. He leaves the burnt edges to one side and doesn't say the word 'chocolate' once.

Gran has been out, so I haven't had a chance to talk to her about the Owens until now. I've found the silver-backed comb and I've brought it down, just in case.

'Did you know them, Gran?' I lean my head on her knees, as she untangles my hair before bed.

'Yes. I know them.'

'And did Mrs Owens really go off and leave the children?'

'She did.'

'Why?'

'I don't know about that!' Gran drags the comb roughly through. 'This hair of yours, Helen, is a disgrace.'

'But Dad said . . .'

'My little Edith, or your great Auntie Edith, as she would have been, she would never have let her hair get like this!'

'About the Owens, Gran. Dad said –'

'Your father, he says too much!'

'Then tell *me*, Gran.'

'What is there to tell? The mother, Mrs Owens, she only came to me the night before. She wanted the loan of the train fare, though I knew I'd never see that money again! She was always trying to borrow, always asking me for things that I cannot give. A cup of sugar, half a loaf for the children's tea.'

'Did you lend her the money, Gran?' But I already knew.

'No!'

'What did she do?'

'Nothing! She left my kitchen, like a rat leaving a ship, and never even said goodbye. She was not a good woman. Not at all.'

'So that was the end of it, after she'd gone?'

'The end? No! It was the beginning, because no sooner had the mother gone than the daughter started to come round. "Please, Mrs Kopperberg, Dad says can we borrow a piece of cheese, a jug of milk, five pounds until tomorrow?" There she was, morning and night, like a black little cat, whining at my door. With those eyes of hers so –'

'That'd be Sam.'

'And such a stupid name for a girl!' Gran tugs at a knot and makes me flinch.

'It's short for Samantha.'

'You think *that* makes it a proper name? There were never "Samanthas" when I was young. Oh, but she was a sly one. A black-eyed hussy, through and through.'

'What do you mean? She was only a little girl.'

'Never! She was never a little girl; always hanging around on the street at night, sitting on the seawall, swinging her legs, waiting outside the public houses, letting the fishermen buy her chips. And I don't know what else.'

'I never knew that.'

'Of course you didn't! Do you think I would let you out at night? Oh no. I took care of you both.' She leans close. 'And with Tom around too –'

'With Tom around?' I prompt.

'Well, I have to be extra careful, don't I?'

'Why?'

'Why!' She frowns. 'You don't know *why*? Your mother lets you walk around half naked and she doesn't tell you about these things?'

'What things?' My heart beats as if I'm standing on the edge of a cliff.

'He was young, your brother, but almost a man, and she was never a child. Not her, with her black eyes and her dirty hair. And there she was, coming round every day, wanting to sit in my kitchen, wanting to talk! Well, I couldn't have that. She wasn't *my* child.'

I see Sam at the door. She would have pushed back her hair and said 'hello'. And Tom would have looked up, and smiled.

'What did you do, Gran?'

'I tell David Owens that he must look to his daughter.'

'So what happened?'

'Nothing. What should happen? Do you think I am afraid of David Owens? Never. And that girl never bothers me again. Her father saw to that.'

'I bet he did.' I remember the photo of David Owens with his hands clamped over the shoulders of the two children and I don't know what to say. Gran sighs, and combs on, until my hair is soft and smooth. Then she kisses me and I go up to bed.

'Helen!' Luke whispers as I pass his door later.

'What is it? Why aren't you asleep?'

'Helen, Chris said they'd seen you. You and Wiffy Owens.'

'What!' I click on his bedside light and he ducks away.

'He said you were doing kissing. Together.' His nose wrinkles in disgust. 'Why did you do that, Helen?'

'I didn't! Who told you that?'

'Chris. Chris said –'

'It's a lie!' I didn't mean to shout. Luke stops wriggling and lies still. 'Who is this "Chris" anyway?'

'Nobody,' he says with his eyes tightly shut.

'Who is it? Tell me, Luke.' I shake his shoulder but he twists away and begins to sniff loudly as though he's about to cry.

'It's nobody,' he mutters, through clenched teeth, 'nobody at all.'

Chapter 15

'Pat? Is that you?' The first phone box was out of order so I've come to the one on the main road and now I can barely hear her voice because the rush-hour traffic is thundering past. I've jammed in loads of coins and I don't care what it costs. This is one call I couldn't make at home.

'Pat are you there?'

'Yes! Whatever's the matter, Helen?'

'It's Tom! I've opened his box.'

'What box?'

I hold the receiver away from my ear. She's asking what the matter is again and again but I can't explain. For the first time in our lives it feels as though we are too far apart.

Last night, after talking to Gran, I couldn't sleep. The flame flickered so and I tossed and turned. Sometimes I thought I heard him in the room next door and sometimes I thought it was only Luke, snuffling still in his sleep. Then, I suddenly thought about looking through the rest of Tom's things. It was what I wanted to do, though I didn't know why.

I avoided switching on the light and felt my way into the garage and lifted the box from the stack. I'd intended to look at it down there, to rifle quickly through and flush out the ghosts, like moths from old clothes, but it was too cold. My feet ached on the concrete floor so I took the box back to my room.

I crouched beside it on the window seat with my feet tucked under for warmth. I thought I could just look through his things and remind myself of how he had been. I thought I could keep him safe. I was sure that it would prevent them from stealing him from me. As I opened the box, that's what I thought.

There were magazines on top, and some of his clothes neatly folded. A few pairs of socks were rolled up, because he, unlike me, was tidy. There were some underclothes, his tennis whites, his sunglasses and his collection of baseball caps. There was a magnifying glass and a polythene bag full of keys and marbles and dice and heavy old coins. The rubber band twisted round the neck of the bag had perished. It fell apart when I tried to open it.

I took out one of his frayed cotton shirts. It was cold and damp. I shook it but the creases remained as sharp as the pattern of tiles on a roof. I found his stamp book, some local history magazines and then a pencil case. It was a scruffy red plastic one with tooth marks in one corner: my tooth marks probably. We used to play this game where I was his little dog and scrabbled around on all fours and barked a lot, so I could have bitten it then.

I unzipped it and felt inside amongst the biro caps and crayon ends and the dust of sharpenings, heaped at the bottom. If there was a decent sharpener in there, I thought I'd take it, because mine lets the leads get too long. Tom had had a lucky silver sixpence too, but I didn't find that. Instead, my fingers touched a piece of paper, jammed in one corner, and folded up very small. I fished it out. Pat and I always passed notes at school. We wrote outrageous things because if you only wrote 'what are you doing at break?' the teacher would read it out to the class and you felt like a sad prat. If the notes were too rude, staff just frowned and chucked them in the bin, like tissues full of snot.

I unfolded Tom's note, only it wasn't that at all. It was a letter, pencilled in a child's thick hand. I smoothed out the

120

small sheet of lined paper. I was puzzled. I didn't remember writing letters to him, nor having such a poor hand, but I could just make out a row of kisses at the end and two hearts with an arrow through. So I began to read.

> *Dear Tom,*
>
> *Thank you very much for the Letter and the Photo I like them tons I am Sorry that you Gone Away When you Come Back Next Year I will show you more Things I will Send You my Photo like you ask for but next Week I love you Tom ever so much I always will Tom for ever and ever and ever.*
>
> *Yours Faithfully*
>
> *(Miss) Samantha Owens*
>
> *PS. How is your Back Christian says.*

That's what I found last night, when I looked through the box of his things.

'Helen?' Pat yells. 'Talk to me, or give me the number, at least. Then I can call you back.'

I'm crying so much I can barely read it out and just for a moment I imagine escape. I imagine them jumping into their old van straightaway. 'Come on then!' Rooky'll shout as he hurries down the drive. Pat will scramble in beside him, slinging her sports bag in the back. They'll drive through the night, watching the wet, black miles disappear. They'll cross the Severn Bridge and see the sun rising over the smoking chimneys of Port Talbot. Tomorrow they could be knocking on our door. 'We've come to take Helen away,' they'll say and I'll go. I'll share Pat's double bed again. We'll talk all night and when we wake at midday she'll stretch and rub the sleep from her eyes, as she pushes back her strawberry hair.

'Hey!' Someone raps on the glass.

'I thought it was you.' Christian Owens is peering through. He smiles at me before nodding to a couple of young men who are waiting further down the street. They must have been walking past the telephone box and he must have turned back. I wipe my eyes quickly.

'We're going for a drink,' he says, not noticing, or not minding. 'Would you like to come? It's only to the Nelson.'

'All right.'

I put the receiver back because Pat won't ever come and save me, and even if she does, it'll be too late. We start to walk down the street. Behind us the phone rings. He looks at me but I don't turn round or hesitate. I shrug and smile at him and I flip back my hair. I don't want to go back. Not now.

It's busy and loud in the pub and I guess that most of the men must be from the dock. I've been in pubs with Mum and Dad and we've had meals, and Pat and I went once on our own. I didn't have a problem getting served because I've always looked older than I am, but we didn't stay long. We didn't know what to do after we'd had our drinks, so we left. This is the first time I've been in a pub on my own and I'm still not sure how to behave.

'Good health!' He lifts his glass. His companions, who have remained by the bar, watch me as they drink. Then they look away.

I say 'cheers' and take a gulp. I don't like cider but I'd never say. It usually tastes of glue but this is ice-cold so not too bad, which is lucky because it's a large glass.

Christian is wearing shorts and as we sit down at one of the tables his knee touches my leg.

He says something I don't catch because the door swings open and a crowd of people comes in. I nod, as if I had

122

heard, and I drink some more. He moves along and is so close that his shoulder is against mine.

'Is Wiffy enjoying the book?' I ask. I can't think what else to say.

'What book?'

'*Tom*'s book.' Somehow, I can't explain.

'Tom?' he's puzzled.

'Yes! My brother Tom, the one who . . .' I take another gulp. 'Hasn't my mother said?'

'Said what?'

'About Tom.'

'No. Juliet hasn't said a thing. But *you* have.'

'When?' I'm suddenly confused. I can't believe that Mum hasn't talked about Tom.

'When you fainted that day. "Stop, Tom" was what you said. So what is it about Tom?'

'It's just . . .'

'Just?' He's waiting but it's too hot in the pub and I feel giddy. Crying can make you giddy, if you let it, though I never do. I can cry for ever and never let it show.

'Helen?' He reaches round and touches my cheek. 'Helen? What's this?' He's wiped off a tear.

'Nothing.' I look away, because I can't look into his face.

I'm blushing, burning and melting with shame. Sweat is running down me and it'll show on my shirt. I try to undo another button but his hand is in the way.

Then the pub door bangs back as someone pushes in. People move aside and the barmaid reaches down a glass tankard from a hook.

'Evening, Glyn,' she says as she fills it up.

Glyn Owens drinks straightaway, sucking in gulps while the foam is still trickling over the rim. I know I shouldn't be watching him.

123

'Well, well!' He pushes his way across. 'The beautiful Helen! Again.' Then he tilts his head back as though for a better view. He narrows his eyes and sinks his mouth over the thick, rough edge, and drinks again. His long red tongue is distorted by the glass but as our eyes meet he moves it about. I look away and start to drink, but wipe my mouth instead.

'The beautiful Helen!' His voice is louder than before.

People turn and stare.

'The face that launched a thousand ships –'

'Leave it, Glyn.' Christian stands up.

'What's that?' Glyn's lips smile, but not his eyes.

'I said leave her alone.'

'Pardon me! Am I getting too close?' Glyn Owens takes a stride back and opens his arms in mock despair. 'Forbidden, is it, for a poor fisherman to look at Helen of Troy?'

Nobody speaks.

'Didn't know *that*, did you, young Christian, that Miss Troy here launched a thousand ships? Still with a beautiful face like that, and –' He sculpts the hour-glass of tits and bum and beer slops from the tankard in his hand.

I stand up, but I shouldn't have, because as soon as I'm on my feet Glyn is staring at the damp place where I've undone the button after all.

'Come on,' Christian puts a hand on my elbow to steer me through the confusion of tables and stools and people standing too close. It's difficult to focus and I stumble over someone's feet.

'Ooopsadaisy, Miss Troy!' Glyn Owens grabs my hand. 'Launched the boats, then drowned the men! That's what our Helen did, the mucky bitch!' Glyn has stepped too close.

'Come on,' Christian urges but I can't move because Glyn is holding my hand.

'She covered the surface of the sea with the faces of dead men, that's what my old Dad always said, but you don't want to hear that, do you, Christian? And I've been wondering why. And now I've seen your Helen, I'm wondering if I can guess the answer to that riddle. Shall I, Christian? Shall I make a guess?' He raises my hand to his mouth. I can't stop him and don't even try, but he doesn't kiss my hand. He lifts it high above my head, then suddenly lets it drop.

Outside it's cold. A breeze is blowing off the water.

'I'm sorry about that. I should never have taken you in there.'

'It doesn't matter.' I'm standing on the edge of the quay.

'And you're shivering.' He pulls off his red sweater.

'It doesn't matter,' I shrug once more, but I take his sweater and, as I drag it over my face, I smell his warmth within.

'But what did your uncle mean?' I ask, pulling it down.

'Nothing!' He answers quickly. 'He was drunk. He didn't mean anything at all. Come on, I'll take you back.'

I follow him in silence along the cliff path. There's no flame tonight and it's almost too dark to see, but I'm aware of him, just ahead.

'About Tom,' he says, as I open the garden gate.

'What about him?' I'm rude and stupid and I turn away. 'He died. That's all.'

'He *died*? You mean, that boy, your brother is dead?'

'That's right!'

'But –'

I run awkwardly up the path, because I don't want to go at all. I wanted him to take my hand, and put his mouth on mine. I wanted him to hold me so close to him that I couldn't have thought about anything else at all.

Chapter 16

'Excuse me, ladies!' Mrs Cable has run over during lunch break. I've been walking round the outside of the netball courts with Mandy and some other girls from my tutor group. I've been avoiding Samantha who is walking round in the opposite direction, but on her own. Sometimes she's tried to catch my eye but I've pretended that I haven't seen a thing.

'I don't want to spoil your fun,' Mrs Cable continues, 'but I've got to borrow Helena for a moment, if that's all right.' She's holding up her arms, as if I'm some unruly animal which she has to separate from the herd and steer away. 'This way, dear,' she says.

I'm annoyed at myself but I go. Next time, I'll refuse. I'll tell her that I'm not their tame counsellor. I'm not my Dad, doing his charity thing. My brother's death doesn't mean that I understand anything at all.

The girls pull faces and step aside before regrouping and walking on.

'What's she done?' Samantha yells suddenly from the far side.

'Nothing!' I shout back but when I glance at Mrs Cable's face I know that I'm wrong.

'The thing is, Helena,' Mrs Cable closes the white room door. This time, there's no tearful student hanging over the basin, sniffing and waiting for me, and suddenly I wish there was. 'Helena, dear –'

'I'm Helen. My name's *Helen*, Mrs Cable, not *Helena*.'

'Is it dear? Why didn't you say?'

'I did.'

'Well, *Helen*. Is that how you'd like me to say it?'

'Yes.'

'Very well, dear. If that's what you want. And maybe it explains something about last Friday, Helen.'

I think back: Friday had been a normal school day. It was the day after I found Sam's letter to Tom. It was the evening I'd phoned Pat.

'Last Friday, Helen, somebody saw you in the Nelson public house. They saw you drinking.' She's nervous and I stare fixedly over her head, which isn't difficult when you're as tall as I am.

'I wasn't there myself because I don't, as a rule, drink. Perhaps a sherry at Christmas or something in milk, if I can't sleep, but that's not drinking, is it?'

I don't return her smile because this feels like war.

'You, Helen, are under age, although people could easily think otherwise, especially men.'

I hold my breath.

'My friend saw a very unpleasant incident, almost a fight and when he told me about it, I put two and two together and recognized you, Helen, as the girl.'

I still wait.

'You're a very striking girl, Helen.' She glances awkwardly at me, so that we both know exactly what she means. 'And with a name like that, well.'

I want to toss back my hair and light up a fag and snarl. She's wrong. She's being absurdly unfair. I want to scream 'So what!' I want to mock her and ask what she thinks she can do about it. I want to explain that it wasn't my fault, to prove that her remark is outrageous. I want her to stammer and blush and turn away. But I'm not brave and I just look at the floor.

'It isn't what you think, Mrs Cable. Christian's a friend of the family. He was a friend of my older brother when they were both boys and that's what he is to me, Mrs Cable. He's like an older brother. That's all.'

'Is he, Helen?'

'Yes! What else could he be?'

She doesn't answer. She shakes her head in a disbelieving sort of way. I ignore it and look at the hot red bar above. And I wait.

She's frightened me though, and my legs feel weak and my heart pounds unpleasantly as I walk away.

'Had a go at you, did she?' Samantha has been waiting for me and I'm glad. She doesn't ask me what was said and I don't tell her. We just walk round and round together, until the bell rings for afternoon registration, and we have to go in.

When I get home after school the telephone is ringing. I run past Gran and pick it up.

'Pat?' I gasp.

'No. It's Mum.'

'Mum? What's up?'

'Nothing. Why should anything be up? I'm only phoning to tell you that I'll be late.'

'That's fine. I'll tell –'

'Juliet! Where are you?' Dad runs straight in from the garden and snatches the phone from my hand.

They're shouting at each other, then Dad bangs the receiver down and goes into his office and shuts the door.

'Look at that!' Gran turns to me. 'He was wearing his boots. He has made the muddy marks on the floor!'

He looks up when I take in a mug of tea.

'She said she'd be late.' His voice is trembling. His head is buried in his hands. 'She says there's a couple of hours extra work at the garden centre.'

'So?' I don't see what the big deal is. I couldn't care less what she does. I don't care if she's late.

'Why's she doing this, Helen?' Dad and I stare at each other across his desk. 'We don't need the money. It's not as if the work's interesting! So why?' He takes his glasses off, and blows his nose. 'It's *him* isn't it?'

'Who?'

'It's that blasted Christian Owens.'

I don't know how to reply.

'That's why she's working late. She wants to be with *him*.' He's angry, rather than hurt.

'Maybe,' I shrug. I want to get away.

'I knew it! The moment she started talking about him, I knew something was wrong.'

'What do you mean, Dad?'

He doesn't answer straight away.

'Your mother's sick of me, Helen, and of us.'

I shrug. I can't believe he's only just noticed.

'She's going to leave me, Helen. She's going to start again, with someone new. Someone young enough to be her son!'

'What?' I shout.

'Your mother's . . .' He looks at me with hopeless, disbelieving eyes.

'No!' I'm not going to let him even think of it, let alone say it. It's revolting. I've never heard anything so gross and disgusting in all my life.

'No, Dad! You've got it totally wrong. She isn't interested in him like *that*. This isn't about you and her, or even *us*. It's about *Tom. That's* why she's so interested in Christian Owens.' I watch his face and I see that he still hasn't understood. 'She thinks he can be another *son*!'

'She *what*?' Colour suddenly floods his pale face.

'She does, Dad, honestly. She even said so to Luke. She

129

said that he was going to be a "new brother". And it's so pathetic, Dad, and so unfair, and she hasn't got any right because nobody can replace Tom. Never!'

'Tom?' He shakes his head. He still hasn't understood what I've said, and I'm not sure that he's even heard me. So I just rush on.

'Yes! Tom! You've got it wrong, Dad, absolutely wrong, and I can prove it.'

'How?' He's begging me and his eyes are wet.

'Christian isn't interested in *Mum*. How could he be? She's too old! She's the same age as his mother, like you said.'

'That doesn't mean anything.'

'It does! And anyway, I happen to know that he's in love with someone else, someone *young*.'

'Who?'

'Me.'

'*You*!' He stares at me, as though I'm mad.

'Why not?'

He doesn't say a word. He looks me up and down, and I hate him for not believing me.

'It's true. That's where I was yesterday evening, Dad. I meet Christian Owens, after school. He's crazy about me and he's taking me out.' I take a deep breath. 'And on Friday we went to the pub. You can ask anybody you want. They all saw us there. And I drank.'

'You did *what*?'

'I know you'll think I shouldn't have, but I did.' I wait for him to explode but I should have known better than that.

He lets out a long sigh and claps his hands to his head. I wait for the onslaught and for him to tell me that the Owens are a bad and wicked lot, but he doesn't. He begins to smile.

'Oh my,' he brushes the tears from his eyes, 'what a mess!

How blind and stupid can one man be? Especially a father, eh?'

I'm still waiting for him to be angry with me. He should be warning me against the Owens and begging me not to get involved. He should be telling me to stay clear of them and reminding me of the past, but he doesn't. He shakes his head, finishes his tea and blows his nose. Then he jumps up, and stretches his arms above his head as though a great weight has been lifted from him and he is now free.

'God, what a fool I've been, Helen, no wonder Christian Owens wanted to be pleasant to your old mum. It's because of *you*. He's been softening her up! It's the oldest trick in the world.' Dad looks me up and down in the same way that Mrs Cable did, and I despise him, which I've never done before.

'You've grown up, Helen, and I've never noticed. I thought you were still a little girl. But you're not are you? Not any more.'

I smile, but I want to disappear.

'The thing is, Helen, I've done something really stupid. It's something I shouldn't have done at all.'

'What, Dad?' I don't want to know.

'I told your mother that Luke was sick again. I told her that she had to come back at once because he was really ill.'

Downstairs the doorbell rings. For one moment I let myself imagine that it's Rooky and Pat, come to take me safely away.

'That'll be her!' He leaps up, then stops. 'You go, Helen. I can't. Not yet.'

It isn't Mum and it isn't Rooky and Pat either. It's Gran, and she's angrily calling my name.

Chapter 17

'Helen!' Gran is shouting across the hall. She's holding up the corner of a polythene bag as if there is something disgusting inside but I can see that it's only Tom's book.

'Who brought that back?' I run to the front door.

'Someone. I don't know who.' Gran's lying and not bothering to conceal it. I race into the front garden but it wasn't Christian. It was Sam. I run to the road and call her name.

'You can't have that girl in this house!' Gran has followed me out. She plucks at my sleeve.

'What girl?' I snap at her. 'I thought you didn't know who it was.'

'I know quite well, thank you. And she is not welcome here.'

'Why not?'

'You *know* why not, Helen. Your father and I have told you. So please.' She tries to take my hand but I pull away and shout over the gate.

Sam turns round. She saunters back and comes up our garden path, then stops in front of Gran. She tosses back her black wing of hair and looks as though she'll spit.

'You didn't really forget me, did you, Mrs Kopperberg?' Her voice is a smoky growl.

Gran doesn't say anything but her eyes are bitter and cold. I never expect old people to look like that. You'd think that hate would die away, but with my Gran it's alive and well.

'Who is it?' Dad comes out of his office and hesitates in the hall.

'I brought the book back, Mrs Kopperberg,' Sam explains. 'Helen lent it to my brother and I've brought it back, that's all.' She's hesitant and almost apologetic. I hadn't expected that either because she must have seen Gran's look of hate.

'Come on up,' I mutter. I want to get away. She's brought a sour smell of smoke and unwashed clothes into the hall and Gran, who disapproves of smokers, has begun to sniff.

'It's the fish, Mrs Kopperberg.' Halfway up the stairs Sam stops and turns back. 'The smell gets everywhere and I can't help it, but I put his book in a bag, just in case. Because I remember, Mrs Kopperberg, how you always liked things nice and clean.'

Gran begins to protest. I hear Dad telling her to be quiet and not to interfere. I quickly shut my bedroom door, so Sam won't overhear.

'Wow!' Sam looks round the room. 'This is so nice. Aren't you lucky, Helen, having a room like this? We don't have anything nice in our house. Not now.' She fingers the carved edge of my wardrobe. 'Did your dad get this for you? He's cute isn't he, with those little specs.' She touches this and that and moves restlessly around. I haven't had anyone in this room before, or not a friend. Somehow, I had always imagined that the person I shared it with would be Pat.

I begin the complicated story of the wardrobe and Pat and Rookie, but she interrupts.

'Do I smell, Helen?'

'No!'

'Are you sure?'

'Yes! You mustn't take any notice of my Gran. She's old now and a bit daft, I think.' I didn't intend to lie but I had to make an excuse.

133

'Is she? I wouldn't have thought that, not of your Gran. She was always such a terror when we were kids and I was frightened of her. I really was.'

'Me too.'

'Were you? I didn't know that. I thought it was just me. But we respected Mrs Kopperberg a lot, or my mum did, and wouldn't have a word said against her. My mum respected your Gran a lot. Well you have to, don't you, when someone's lived through that war like she did. She was in one of those camps in Germany, wasn't she, with all the Jews? She must have been a tough woman, your Gran.'

'A girl, actually. She was only fifteen, and her little sister, Edith, was much younger still. They were only kids.'

'Were they?' Sam seems surprised. 'That's so horrible, isn't it? Where's the little sister now? Somewhere close by?'

'No. She died in the camps. Gran came back alone.'

'That's the worst of all, isn't it? Being the one that's left, and being all on your own.' She laughs and sits down on my bed. 'Like I say, she's as tough as an old eel, your Gran. Though, please, Helen, I don't mean nothing rude, when I say that. She's unlucky, all the same.'

'What do you mean?' I'd always thought that Gran was the lucky one. That's what she'd always said. It was Edith we cried about, not Gran.

'To be the one that's left. That's all I meant.' Sam gets up and moves around, touching things and picking them up, and I wish she'd sit down.

'About that book,' she turns towards me suddenly. 'I looked at it you know and that's why I've come. Really, that's it. I'm not much of a reader, Helen, but I looked at the pictures and they tell you a lot.' She takes it from the bag and begins to flip through. 'And I wondered, Helen, if you know about things like that. And like this, here.' She's opened up a picture of the Minotaur and now she leans across. 'It couldn't ever be, could it, Helen? Do you think there could ever be in the world something like that?'

'Like what?'

'Something what's half animal and yet half a man, like that?' She holds the book towards me and she's watching my face.

It's a photograph of a statue of the Minotaur that has been stuck back together, but not very well. I can see the cracks and where an arm has been joined back beneath the shoulder and where the horns have been broken off. But the bull's heavy head still leers from the shoulders of a man. The forelock is whorled and dense, the eyes, small and mean. I can almost smell the hot, wet sweat and the muck in its rough, tufted hide.

'This Mino-taur,' she traces the name with her finger, 'there couldn't ever be one, could there, not even as a freak?'

'No! It's a sort of story, a myth. It's something someone made up, a long time ago.' I try to close the book but she holds on, and I can almost feel the beast's thick breath.

'Like this?' She turns over to the picture of Leda and the Swan.

I remember how it used to frighten me, years ago. We look at the white swan's webbed feet on Leda's thigh and at its talons curved round and gripping her flesh. Sam runs her finger along the thick feathered neck of the bird as it bends over the girl in its cruel caress.

'Look there,' she points to a part of the swan's curved wing. 'Half close your eyes, Helen, and it's like a man, isn't it, amongst all those feathers. Do you see that?'

I shake my head but I'm shivering.

'I've never liked their dark feet,' I laugh brightly. I don't tell her that they used to remind me of the grainy skin of a toad.

'Oh well,' she laughs too. 'I've never liked swans, either, the dirty, stuck-up brutes. Grown-ups used to tell us that if you annoyed a swan it could run at you and break your arms with a flap of its wings. I don't suppose it's true but I believed it all the same. When I saw swans in the dock, and they do come in, now and again, I can tell you, Helen, I kept well away.'

'My parents said the same thing to me. But these are only stories in this book. They're things people have made up.'

'Is that what they are?'

'Oh yes. Tom knew them all but I've forgotten the details now. It's your Wiffy who really knows.'

She looks up quickly.

'That's why I lent him the book. He's interested in stuff like this, isn't he? And I wanted to help. I thought he might like to know more.'

'Did you?' She frowns, as if she doesn't believe me, and continues to leaf through. 'You don't want to listen to Wiffy.'

'Why not?'

'He knows too much, or too little, and he's stupid, so you shouldn't believe anything he says. And anyway, Helen, he makes things up.'

'Like what?'

She doesn't answer me but shuts the book up, reaches into her pocket for a cigarette, then looks up.

'Perhaps I shouldn't, with your Gran and her blood-hound's nose downstairs?'

'Perhaps not.' I feel awkward. 'I'm sorry about that.'

'I don't mind. Honestly. I'm used to it now.' She gets up and moves restlessly around, before returning to the book.

'But you know what they mean by these stories, don't you, Helen?'

136

'Yes.'

But I don't, and I don't want to think about it either. I just want her to go.

'Look, I'll get us some tea.'

'Can I help?' She jumps up and comes to the door.

'No!' My voice is too loud, and she backs away.

'Don't worry, Helen. I won't come down. I know your Gran doesn't think much of me. She never did. And maybe she's not so wrong.'

The television is on in the sitting room. Gran will be in there with Luke. He will be snuggled against her, watching a cartoon. I envy him and, for a moment, I want to join them but I can't. So I make the tea and take the mugs back to my room.

'I see you've got lots of pictures of him.' She's taken my photograph album from the bookshelf over my bed. 'There, that's him isn't it? That's Tom, when he was just a little kid. I'd know him anywhere.'

'Would you?'

Pat hadn't: she never recognized him, until I'd pointed him out.

'Oh yes! I'd know Tom. Handsome, wasn't he, even as a kid?'

She's bending over a photograph of him, taken when he was only four or five. He's on his scooter but looking back over his shoulder, frowning slightly against the sun. His fair hair has tumbled across his forehead and she's right. He was handsome even then.

'I had that scooter later,' I say.

'Did you?' She doesn't look up. Her fingers lightly stroke across the page and I want to tell her that she'll spoil the photos. I want to tell her to stop.

'Yes, I did. It was a present. He painted it bright yellow

for me and the wheels were silver. It was my favourite toy, even though it was old. We called it my "chariot" and I really thought it was.'

She is turning another page.

'I used to scoot along the pavement outside our house, and there was this dog, in another house on the corner. I think it was a red setter. It was called Dandy and it used to bark at me. I always thought it was going to leap over the gate and attack me. I was *so* scared of that dog.'

'Me too,' she says, 'I was so scared I used to wet my pants.'

'You were scared of a dog?'

'No. Not of a dog.'

Then I realize that she's hardly heard a word I've said. She's turning page after page, looking for pictures of Tom. She's not interested in me at all and I wonder if she ever was.

'Where's that?' she asks at last.

'It's the recreation ground. It was at the back of our house. It was ever so nice and in summer we played there a lot.'

'We played too,' she murmurs under her breath.

'You and Christian?'

'No. Not me and Christian, nor Wiffy either.' She's staring at a picture of Tom and me beside the bike-cart. 'In fact, Christian and me and Wiff didn't hardly ever play at all. Our dad saw to that.'

'So who did you play with?'

She gets up and looks out of my window.

'Tom. Like I said, always and only Tom.'

'What did you play?' I try to drink some tea.

'This and that, kid's stuff really. And I showed him things . . .'

'What things?' I whisper, tilting the mug this way and then that.

'Things from the sea, things from wrecks. You find all

138

sorts of stuff washed up on the beaches here, especially after a storm.'

'So that's *all* you did?'

'No. That's not all. We kissed, didn't we, and –'

'But you couldn't have!'

'Why not? I loved Tom.'

'You didn't! You were a child. Children don't fall in love.'

'Don't they?'

'No!'

'Well, we did.'

'You *didn't*. You couldn't have or I'd have known. Anyway, you called him a coward that day on the beach and you wouldn't have done that if you loved him!'

'Why not?' She asks.

I can't answer her because I don't understand. I want her to go, to leave my room and this house, and never ever come back.

'I was jealous,' she says. 'That's why I said it.'

'Jealous? Why were you jealous?'

'I was jealous of you, of course. That's why.'

'Of me?'

'Well, yes.' She scrapes at something with her nail. 'You had him all the time, didn't you, Helen? From morning till night and every single day of your life, and I didn't have anything at all. Or only now and then, and from a distance because your Gran wouldn't have me in her house. Not that I blame her, not really. But I did blame you. Because you were always there, weren't you, getting in the way? You were always hanging around and tagging along. That's why I pushed you, Helen. I was so jealous of you then.' She stands up quickly. 'I wanted you to fall in. Not to drown, mind you, but just to get a good scare. I know I shouldn't have wanted that, but I'm afraid I did.'

139

I can't speak.

'I suppose I'd better go now?' Her voice isn't angry. It's sad.

I keep staring out to sea and I don't turn round until she's left. When I hear the front door slam, I open my window as wide as I possibly can. I see myself out there on the beach again, tagging along.

'Helen?' Later, Luke puts his head round my door. 'Has she gone?'

'Yes.'

'Good.' He scrambles on to my bed and jumps.

'Why good?' As if I didn't know.

'Gran says she's a wicked liar and a wicked, wicked witch!' He jumps higher each time.

'Does she say that?'

He nods vigorously.

'What else does she say?'

'She says that girl smells.'

I don't say anything. I just know that Gran is wrong.

Chapter 18

'Helen, wake up!'

I don't open my eyes. I want to wriggle down to somewhere warm but Luke is pulling the edge of the duvet further back.

'Helen, please get up.'

I've either overslept or Luke has come in way too early because he's already dressed for school. He's combed and clean and, since the sun is streaming through the open window, it must be me who's out of step.

'Dad says hurry up because it's half-past.' He smells of toothpaste as he leans close and examines my face. I wonder if the dream that is now seeping away from me has left its trace. I sit up and shiver in the cold room. I lick the sour surface of my nasty, uncleaned teeth and the dream vanishes as hopelessly as snow held in the palm of your hand.

'Helen, why did you sleep in your clothes?'

I frown, because despite the sweaty bundle of school things, rucked up around me, I'm actually freezing cold. Then I remember. Last night I had waited for Mum to come back. I had sat by the open window watching the flame and listening for the sound of her key. Dad must have been doing the same because he got to the front door long before me. From the top of the stairs I saw him fling his arms around her as though she had been missing for weeks and was now found. He was kissing her neck. She asked him what was up and she tried to fend him off. When he started to murmur her name, I went back to my room. I had paused in the doorway. I wanted to hear her ask how Luke was. When she didn't, I quickly closed my door, and lay on my bed.

A few minutes later I heard her quick step on the stairs but she didn't go to Luke's room. She didn't even open the door and peep in. I heard Dad calling her back but she wasn't listening to him. She burst in on me, switched on my light, told me that I was a stupid little girl who didn't know what I was doing and had better stop it right now. She leant over me and there were red blotches of anger, high up on her cheeks. Dad had just told her that I'd been seeing Christian Owens, so she had to tell me that it was the most absurd bit of rubbish she'd ever heard in her whole life.

'Your father says you got him to take you to a pub. For goodness sake, Helen, whatever possessed you, or him? He's almost twice your age, apart from anything else.'

'He isn't.'

'Well, maybe not exactly, but that isn't the point, is it? You may look grown up, but you're not. You're still a child. And I shall tell that to Christian tomorrow. It's so ridiculous.'

'It isn't.'

'So, what is it then, Helen? Would you like to tell me what's going on?'

I wanted to, but I didn't. I wanted to say things that would make her mouth open with shock and outrage, and then I wanted her eyes to narrow with envy as she listened, but I couldn't say a thing.

'Well?' She put her hands on her hips.

'Nothing's going on,' I pulled a stupid, childish sort of face. She waited and I stared at the patterns in the carpet, until she was gone. Then I had kicked off my shoes and climbed straight into bed. I had dragged the duvet over my face. Since I couldn't curl up and die, I shut my eyes as tightly as I could and must have finally gone to sleep. But I had dreamt about him in the night and would have been dreaming still, if Luke hadn't come in.

'Helen,' he begins to giggle and hops from foot to foot. 'Helen, I'm sorry. I know it was a secret but I've sort of told Dad.'

'What?'

'That, that –' He's laughing too much. It's spilling between the fingers of the hand that's clapped over his mouth. If it wasn't so late, I'd pull him into bed and cuddle him half to death.

Outside my open window it's a brilliant autumn morning. Gulls are calling and the sky is clear and blue.

'Go on,' I plead, 'you can tell me, can't you?' To me the air feels raw and cold, and I wouldn't have minded hearing a silly, childish joke.

Downstairs Mum's already gone to work. Dad is busy with toast. Luke is fiddling in the corner of the room, waiting for me. Gran looks at her watch and gives a sigh to remind us that she and Edith were never allowed to be late. Then she insists that Dad drives us to school. I can't refuse because Luke is already scampering towards the car. I follow, although I wouldn't have minded being late. Dad doesn't speak to me until we've dropped Luke off at the gate, then he clears his throat.

'You mustn't take too much notice of your mother, Helen.' He's gripping the wheel very tight. 'I think it's all been rather a shock to her.'

'What has?'

'*You* have. And this thing, between you and young Christian Owens. What I mean is, she hadn't noticed that you'd, well . . .'

'Grown up?'

'Something like that.'

'Only it isn't like that, Dad.'

'Isn't it?' He laughs awkwardly. 'It's all right, Helen, *I* understand even if your mother doesn't, or not yet.'

But he doesn't either, and he's not going to try.

'Luke told me this morning that he'd seen you kissing along the cliff path.'

'That's not true!'

'Like I say, it's nothing to be ashamed of.' He stops the car in front of the school.

'About the Owens, Dad.'

'Actually, Helen, I wanted a word about that, too. I haven't just made a fool of myself over your mother. I think I've been a bit hasty about the Owens as well! I've listened to too many of your Gran's stories, I expect. Whatever happened with the Owens – and nothing was ever proved, mind you – it was all a very long time ago.' He frowns and pushes his glasses back up. 'And one shouldn't listen to gossip, should one?' He's drumming his fingers on the steering wheel, waiting for me to agree, but I can't. It isn't what I want to hear. I want him to ask me to be careful. I want him to warn me off, but he doesn't. He keeps on drumming his fingers on the wheel as he tells me that he doesn't want to stand in my way. Then he leans across and opens the passenger door and waits for me to get out.

The second bell must have already rung because the late-comers are hurrying in for registration. They're streaming across the road in front of the car and, as Dad's still waiting for me, I have to get out. I can barely drag my feet across the tarmac, towards the door, and when I stop, they all swarm past.

'Not coming in?' Only Wiffy has turned back. I shrug, but as our eyes meet, I'm already shaking my head.

144

'Is Sam in school?'

He laughs and pulls a face.

'Is she at home then? Helping your mum?'

He laughs even more. He tips his head back, and laughs out loud, and he's still laughing as I walk away down the path.

I knock again and again at the Owens' house. Nobody answers at first, but a door opens upstairs and I hear an unwilling step coming down. It isn't Sylvia who undoes the latch. This time it's Sam. Her legs are bare and she's pulling a sweater quickly down. I've woken her up.

'Yes?' She yawns and rubs her eyes.

'I've got something to tell you, something I forgot to say last night.'

She looks at me suspiciously, and yawns again.

'It's about Tom.'

'Is it?' She pushes back her hair then, and lets me come in.

She shows me into the best room, or at least that's what I think it is. It's cold and as soon as she opens the door I can tell that it's been shut up. There's a scrappy bit of cut-off carpet, in the middle of a black-painted floor. Its ends are frayed and curled up, like stale sliced bread. A set of black shelves, with almost nothing on them but dust, is propped against the wall by bricks. There's a large red plastic arm-chair by an empty grate. Cigarette burns pock its arms, and the back is smeared grey with the grease from someone's head. Three cardboard boxes of empty bottles are partly covered by a bit of torn sheet.

'Bit chilly, isn't it?' Sam pulls her sweater further down. She hesitates. She tries to draw back from the room but I push her on.

'No! It's not a bit cold, it's fine! And what a great chair!' I sit down with a thump, and try to swing round. It's the ugliest room I've ever seen and I'm glad.

145

'Don't sit there,' she says.

I jump up and perch awkwardly on the edge of a shabby pink sofa opposite, with a scarf, or something, stretched over a stain.

'This is *so* nice.' I speak loudly when I should have said nothing at all.

'Shall I light a fire?' She hasn't sat in the red chair either, but on the sofa next to me.

' You could do!' I remark brightly, though there's nothing to light a fire with and just the threads of spiders' webs blowing in the grate.

'You had something to tell me, Helen.' She's scraping something on her thigh, with a long dirty nail.

'Yes, but I'm not sure you'll want to hear this.'

'Won't I?' She pulls the sweater towards her knees.

'It's about Tom, though.' I watch with satisfaction as her face lights up. She almost smiles.

'Is it? Is it really?' She pushes back her hair and looks at me, and I smile back. I wonder if she ever thinks about the letter that she wrote.

'It's about how he died. Do you want to hear that?'

She nods and makes a sound that is like dust.

'Well, it was a van.' My voice is hard and clear.

She's picking at her nails now and I think they'll break.

'We were together, Tom and I, and crossing the road from the recreation ground behind our old house. You remember that photo?'

She nods and picks.

'So I suppose Tom wasn't paying attention – not that I was, but I was only *seven*, so it wasn't my fault. It was evening, too, and at the end of a long, hot day. The sun was low, that's what everybody said. And we'd played all day, him and me.' I glance at her but she just picks. 'So in the evening, when we

146

were going home, he stepped out into the road. That's all it was, Sam. He went splat, like a melon. Though actually he flew up in the air first.'

She shivers, and pulls the dirty old sweater down. I don't take any notice. I don't see why I should.

'I still don't know how the van missed me, but it did, so Tom must have been further out. It hit him, and he flew up in the air and fell across the bonnet, then must have got caught, because he was dragged along, underneath.' I watch her. 'For quite a long way.'

'Don't.' She shifts towards me on the sofa, and I smile.

'So, I ran after, and looked, and called his name. And –'

'And?' she takes a small, gasping breath.

'And there he was, all twisted up! And I remember thinking how *small* he was. Like something dropped. And –'

'Don't, Helen, please!' She puts out her hands. 'Don't tell me any more.'

'Why ever not? I don't mind at all. It was ages ago, anyway, and it doesn't upset me now. Unless someone asks, I don't think about it at all.'

'But I do, Helen. I think about it all the time.'

'Why?' I want to hurt her as much as I can. 'He wasn't *your* brother. He wasn't anything to you!'

'Oh, but he *was* Helen. I loved Tom and, just for a summer, he loved me.' She pushes back her hair and looks at me again.

'Anyway,' my voice is too loud, in this desolate room, 'he had loads of other girlfriends! They were queuing. As soon as we got back home from that holiday, they were lining up. He used to meet them in the recreation ground after dark!'

'We all do that,' she wipes her eyes, 'but it doesn't make any difference, does it? It doesn't change how you feel in your heart.'

147

I jump up. Now I want to go.

'Sam!' Someone shouts loudly and bangs on the floor above. She starts but doesn't get up. They bang again.

'Is that your mum?'

'No. She's gone again.'

But someone is coming down the stairs and I want to get away. I've never done anything like this before and I don't want anyone else to know.

'Well, I'll be damned!' Glyn Owens throws back his head and laughs in my face, as he opens the door. 'Little Miss Troy!' He scratches himself slowly, underneath, and then he pushes past. He rubs against me, with his bare chest, and he farts. I step quickly out of reach and he laughs again. He puts his hand on Sam's dark head and, as I watch, he turns it slowly round.

'Helen, don't go! Please!' Her voice is so faint that I pretend I haven't heard, as I run out of the house.

Dad's car is not in the drive and Gran is not pleased when I push open the kitchen door.

'Whatever's the matter now?' she asks, as though she can read it on my face. 'Is it Luke? Has something happened to him in school?'

'It's not Luke.'

'What is it then? Were you too late?'

'It's not Luke and I wasn't even late. It's the Owens, Gran!' I'm shouting at her, though I don't know why. She bends over the sink, and continues washing out a cup. Then she turns round.

'*Always* it is the Owens!' Her anger astonishes me. 'I do not want to *hear* about the Owens! Am I to have no peace? They are the scum of the earth, these people, Helen, and their houses are the nests of rats! That's what I tell your father, Helen, but will he listen to me? No! Times have

148

changed, he says, and I must hold my tongue. I tell him that people never change, but your father is so stupid, sometimes, even though he is my son!'

'Gran!'

'And then he lets that girl in here last night. Lets her slink through our door and crawl up our stairs, so that the whole house stinks! Lets her go into your room, as though she could ever be a friend to you!'

'Gran!'

'Whatever is he thinking of, your father?' The tendons of her neck are stretched like wire and her face is as hard as old, cracked stone. 'And your mother too! Have they no care?'

'Then tell me about the Owens, Gran.'

'No! Never!' Her hair stands up in thick, white tufts, and her eyes are muddy and chilled, like puddles in a thaw.

'Why didn't you help Sylvia Owens, when she came to you, all those years ago?'

'You want to know too much! First the Owens, then –' she breaks off as though she has suddenly remembered something else.

'Then Edith? Yes, that's what I want to know!' I don't know why I say it, but her face crumples, and she grips the edge of the sink.

'Edith?' she repeats, putting the cup back in the water. 'What is there to tell you about Edith, that you have not already heard?' Her voice softens again, as though some danger has passed. 'Such a good skater, was my Edith, in winter, on the frozen dykes –'

'Not *that* story, Gran.'

'Well then, there was her lovely hair.' She unties her apron and tries to hang it on the hook, but drops it on the floor. I reach down, and hand it back.

'I know about that, Gran. I know that she brushed it one

149

hundred times every night, and even in the camp.'

'So, what is it that you want to know?' She steps away from me and folds her arms across her chest. Her old, veined hands are hidden away, like claws, beneath a tattered wing.

'I want to know how she died.'

'And I want to forget!' Her sudden, dreadful rage terrifies me as it used to do, years ago.

'Gran?'

'And do you know why I can't?' she cries. 'It is because of people like *them*, Helen. Always putting their heads round our doors, asking and asking for help that I cannot give.'

Chapter 19

The dock is bright and busy. People are strolling about in the autumn sun and I join them, looking at this and that. They must be the last tourists before winter, because this is a beautiful part of the world, with its silver sea, and its tipped, red cliffs and the gulls wheeling and calling above. That's how I'd describe it, if anybody asked me, and I wouldn't be telling a lie. It is so beautiful here. When you half shut your eyes you needn't see the flame at all, nor the smoke. I stand still and look up. There is a faint trail of it in the sky but the brisk autumn breeze is blowing it away. If you couldn't smell it, you wouldn't know that it's there.

I buy some chips and idle away more time in the sun. Men are working on the quay. I loiter amongst them, and step over the coils of rope, and in between the crates and heaps of nets. I lean against bollards and watch what they do. In front of me, the green-black water laps at the dark wood lining the dock, and ends and bits of things float slowly by. There's a single swan, with its white wings resting back like the caught crest of a wave.

I glance at my watch. In school it's double French now. Wiffy will be nodding off in the front seat and nobody will care. The class will be passing him by because he's a fool. He's the sort of lad who never learns and never knows anything at all. But he knew about Sam, didn't he? He's known all along. That's why he laughed, as if it was some great joke which I was too dumb to understand.

I walk to the furthest corner of the dock. Here, there's no

one about. Piles of rotten pallets, with grass growing between, and drums of this and that, and rusting lengths of massive anchor chain sprawl in the shadow of the old ice-factory. It's cold here and out of the sun but I don't really care.

I want to go back. I want to run up their path and bang my fists on the Owens' front door. It doesn't matter who's there. I'll just push past them and find her. I'll tell her that I'm sorry, and that –

'Helen!' It's Christian. He's climbing awkwardly over the fence behind me, with something in his hand. He hesitates, then waves, and walks across.

'No school today?' He's carrying a carton of milk and a packet of biscuits. He seems surprised to see me but I think he's pleased.

'Oh yes! There's plenty of school,' I shrug.

Does he know too? And if he does, so what! I smile at him. I rest my head against the corrugated wall of the ice-factory and look him up and down.

'There *was* school, but I didn't fancy it. Not today.' I push back my hair and I look at the thin line of his lips, where the cherry pink fades into sunburnt skin, then I look away.

He must know: know and not care.

'Is your boat over there?' I ask brightly, although I can see that it is and that he's watching where I look.

'Helen,' he moves in front but I step aside.

'A green boat is very unusual, isn't it?' I turn back to him, suddenly, and he's so close that I can smell his skin again and see the golden hairs on his wrists. 'Or that's what people say.'

'Do they?'

'Oh yes! They say that a green boat is unlucky, as well, because it's stealing the colour from the sea.'

'Do you believe that, Helen?' He looks towards the *Black*

152

Pig with sudden concern. I remember their father, and wish that I'd kept my big mouth shut, but it's too late now. I shrug again and begin to walk away. He follows me, and at the sea wall I stop and pull myself up. Then I lean back and I slowly swing my legs.

'What else do people say?' he asks, with his free hand on the wall beside mine.

'Nothing! Nothing at all!'

He doesn't believe me and I don't care because he's looking at me as if he is about to take my hand and tell me things I want to hear. When he does, I'll pull him towards me, so that he's holding me very close. When he rests his head on my breasts, I'll bend over him, and put my lips into his hair and I'll find his warm, white skin underneath. Then, in the bright, midday sun, I'll see the shadow of our bodies together, his and mine.

'Can we go on board the *Black Pig*?' I lean towards him and let myself slither down.

'No!' He steps away.

'Why not?' I begin to run towards the boat. He tries to catch hold of me, and keep me back.

'Don't!' I pull free. 'Don't try and stop me, Christian. I'm not a child!'

'Helen!' He calls after me but I take no notice. I run along the pontoon, to where she's moored, and I'm quicker than he is. I climb over the rail on to the shifting deck. The boat sways unexpectedly but I cling on. When I look over my shoulder, he isn't following me. I wave, but he doesn't wave back. I take another step, and below me, in the belly of the boat, something moves. Someone has picked something up and then put it down, shifted a kettle or a pan, maybe, on a stove.

'Hello?' I hadn't expected anyone else to be on board. I step uneasily back.

153

'Hello?' My voice is shaking and I'm holding on. I look round the peaceful, sunlit dock, where the few tourists are watching the trawler men at work. Christian is at the end of the pontoon.

'Is there anyone there?' Nobody answers me, but slowly, stealthily, someone moves.

'Mr Owens?' I breathe, with my heart beating too fast. 'Is that you?'

I make myself walk towards the companion way and then I make myself look down. It's dark inside but I can just see that a kettle has been put to boil in the galley and there are two mugs on the side, but it isn't David Owens who looks up at me from the bunk. It's Mum.

Christian tries to stop me as I push past, but she doesn't say a thing. When I'm far enough away, I stop running and look back briefly, against the sun. I see them standing close together, where he and I should have been. He puts his hand on her shoulder and she doesn't push him away, and all I can think about is poor, stupid Dad.

Above me, in the clear blue sky, white gulls wheel and turn. An ice-cream van is parked on the side of the road and when I leave the dock I join the small queue. Then, I walk towards the cliff path and I lick the chocolate and bite the stiff whirl of vanilla off the top. The breeze has dropped and it's almost as warm as any summer day.

It's always like this, isn't it, when things go wrong? The sun always shines. Pat said that once. We were watching television in her house. It was something awful about floods, and there were pictures of people huddled together on little bits of ground and clinging in trees. All round them, the miles and miles of calm brown water were radiant in the perfect sun.

I push past the holly bush on the bend and step over the

154

gap in the wall. Below, the sea licks the rocks like silk. I pull out Wiff's crooked chair and open it up. It's sheltered here, and warm. After Tom died, those days were perfect too. Every morning after breakfast, I used to run into the garden when the dew was still on the grass, and I'd be planning what we would do. Suddenly, I'd stop in the middle of the lawn, where he and I had ridden round and round on our bikes, and I'd turn back. I'd go up to my room and sit on the edge of the narrow bed and wait, in case I had been mistaken and he was out there after all. I'd shut my eyes and imagine that if I looked out of my window, I'd see him again, standing in the brilliant sun.

I know that I ought to feel outraged, but I don't. I just feel ridiculous and sad. I slump down in Wiff's chair until my head rests more comfortably against the bent bar at the back. I'm shocked and disgusted, too, in a childish sort of way. I didn't want to see that. I didn't want to see her shoulder, bare under the rug, and her clothes in a heap on the floor.

It's warm and sheltered here, and I could almost sleep. Tom and I used to try that in the den but we'd never stayed the whole night. Things rustled and shadows fell across, or I'd been cold, or the moon had been too bright. I used to toss and turn, this way and that, and steal glances at him as he lay asleep. I used to hold my breath and try to stop wriggling and keep still. Then he'd open one eye. We'd start to laugh and be unable to stop because we'd both been awake all along. In the kitchen, he'd heat up soup, in the middle of the night.

But she could have said, couldn't she? Said something to me, or at least not lied.

Behind me someone is walking along the path. They call a child, or a dog, but I don't bother to turn my head. I narrow my eyes and watch the flame in the sky.

At home, Dad will probably be back in his office now. If I push open the door, he may look up, but he won't meet my eye. And now I can't meet his.

'Helen!'

My mouth is dry and the sun has burnt my face.

'Helen!' People are running along the path.

'Helen! Come quick!' Luke screams once more and now I am awake. There are several of them. Luke is on his own, flattened against the wall of brambles and the scrubby bushes with old man's beard and nettles growing in between. The tall boy, the one with the gap teeth, is in front of the others, waving a stick. Luke's face is scarlet. He's gasping as he tries to get his breath. His teeth are bared and his hands held out. When he sees me he suddenly crumples up and begins to cry. Chris Owens starts to whistle through the gap in his teeth. He lowers the stick and grins at me, just like his father had.

'It wasn't my fault, honestly, Helen,' Luke whimpers. He's pushing himself deeper into the thorns, squirming this way and that.

'Yes, it was!' Chris mutters out of the side of his mouth and begins to edge away. One of the children giggles uneasily and looks down. I catch hold of the end of the stick and knock Chris backwards with it, then rip it from his hands. The little ones melt away, then scatter and run.

'Go on then,' Chris shouts, 'go on then, you fat slag! Want to give me one?' He ducks, suddenly and gets free, and although Luke is screaming at me not to leave him, I fling the stick aside and then I run. I catch Chris easily, twist my hand amongst his clothes and jerk him to a stop.

'Touch me, you bitch,' he whines, 'and I'll tell my dad.'

I drag him towards me, step by step, and when he's so close that his body is touching mine, I let him go.

'Go on then, Chris Owens! You go and tell your dad!'

'All right.' He shakes himself and sniffs and rubs his arm where I held on.

'All right, I will.'

'Go on then.'

He doesn't move.

'Go on then!' I give him a push. He stumbles and almost falls. 'But you'd better hurry, because if you don't, I will. As soon as I've taken Luke home, that's what I'm going to do.'

'Don't,' he looks up me. 'Please?'

'Why not?'

'Because –' he rubs the side of his trainer to and fro across a crack in the path. He doesn't need to explain. I see his brown eyes slide with sudden fear and I feel him cringe away from me, just like Wiff.

There's a scratch on Luke's cheek. A curve of bright beads of blood stands out on his skin. I spit on a tissue and dab it off. Then I take his hand in mine and we begin to walk home.

'What wasn't your fault?' I ask as I undo the garden gate.

'Nothing,' he flaps his shoulders up and down, then makes an odd little sound. A plume of yellow vomit streams from his mouth. He whimpers, as if he's been hurt, catches hold of me and throws up again over both our feet.

'Sorry, Helen.' He wipes his mouth.

'That day,' I say slowly, 'when I saw the pirate boat off the Point and you told me that it was the *Black Pig*. Do you remember?'

'No!'

'You'd been kicking stuff about and got your new shoes in such a mess. Tell me about that.'

He shakes his head.

'Tell me!' I pull him to his feet and shake him hard. 'Tell me about that.'

'It wasn't only *me*,' he whines, at last. 'It was *Chris*, too.'

'What was, Luke?' I ask more gently, but I already know.

'It was me that did it, Helen. Chris told me to. He'd said I'd got to do it, and kick everything to bits! Only I didn't know that it was anybody's special little house! Or that boy, Wiffy, would get so mad. And now Chris says that if I don't do what he wants, he's going to tell Wiffy that it was me!' He gulps back tears and looks at me, just like Dad. 'And Gran keeps telling me that the Owens are bad people, Helen, and that their house is full of rats.' He stamps his foot with fury and fear. 'And *that's* why I can't walk along that street, or at least I have to run, because of the rats! And I think Chris has told him anyway and he already *knows*! That's why he's out there, Helen, watching our house!'

'Who is?'

'Wiffy Owens!'

'I don't think Wiffy Owens is watching you.' I put my arms around him, but he pushes me away.

'He *is*! I've seen him in the garden, at night!'

'What's he doing?'

'I don't know!' He stamps his foot again. 'Nothing. Just looking up.'

Chapter 20

Gran is at the kitchen sink when we walk in. We've left our shoes outside the back door, but we must stink because she looks up at once, and sniffs.

'You are sick again?' She feels Luke's forehead and purses her lips. 'It is that packed lunch that your mother gives to you. I tell her, all the time, that a growing boy needs a proper meal in the middle of the day, not always the crisps! But does she listen to me? No!' Gran sighs as she strokes his cheek.

'It isn't Mum's lunches,' I retort, as I peel off my socks. 'Luke's in trouble and he's really upset.'

'What does he have to be upset about? He is only a child!' She frowns. 'And children do not have troubles that make them sick. I've never heard such nonsense, Helen. Troubles are not for children, they are for us.'

'It isn't nonsense, Gran. It's . . .'

She isn't listening to me and suddenly I know she never will. I watch as she turns away and shakes her head. Her old, veined hands are patting his cheek, as if that was ever enough.

I make Luke change. He dawdles, and protests.

'*Helen*,' he drags on my hand again. 'Are you *sure* there aren't rats at Wiff's? Chris says there are *hundreds* in the cellar. He says they're *huge.*'

'Chris Owens is a bully. He only said that to frighten you.' I jerk his sleeve. I want to be gone before Mum gets back.

'But Gran says it *too*.' He threads his hand through the top of the garden gate and hangs on. I have to stop. 'Gran says their house is a *rat's* nest, Helen. Honestly. That's why

159

I have to run!' His voice is very shrill.

'Come on, Luke, please. Come and see for yourself that there aren't any rats.'

He hesitates, but puts his hand in mine. Then we see Mum. She's by herself, on the opposite side of the afternoon street, in the quiet, autumn sun.

'Don't!' I scream at her as she comes across. 'Don't try and say a thing!'

Luke pulls free. He runs over to her and buries his head in her stomach as she begins to cry.

I listen as I walk away from them, but she doesn't call my name.

I stand on the Owens' step, ringing their bell again and again. At last someone comes to the door.

'Helen!' Christian steps away.

I look at him. I glance at his pirate's beard and tied-back, tangled hair. I see the half moon of smooth white skin below his tanned neck, his pale grey, shifting eyes, and his sun-burnt legs.

'Helen! I never –'

'I want to see Sam.' I don't think my voice is too unsteady.

'But –'

'And I want to look in your cellar. I want to see what's down there. People are saying there are rats.'

'Rats? What –?'

I don't take any notice of him. I push past, as if he were any man in the street. I crouch down, catch hold of the ring and heave up the trapdoor.

'Helen!' Wiffy Owens leaps off an old iron bed pushed into one corner. That's all there is down there, the mattress on that bed, the smell of damp and the pictures on the walls. There are hundreds of them. I climb down the steps and am appalled. They are everywhere, hammered and taped and stuck, overlapping, and edge to edge. They cover the bleak cellar walls with another wall of fire.

'What is it, Wiffy? What *is* all this?'

Wiffy tips back his head. Then he points to one of the pictures.

'I like it,' he breathes, coming too close. 'And it keeps me warm. It's all we've got, isn't it, Helen, when we're cold?'

He moves his hand to where the hottest part of the flame would be, and I can't bear to watch, because he's shivering with cold.

'Come on, Wiff.' I push him sharply, but take his hand and lead him up the steps as if he was my child. 'Come on, you need to get out of this rotten place. Let's go up and find Sam.'

'Get out?' He stares at me as I let the trapdoor drop. 'But there's nowhere to go round here! Nowhere at all, except the edge of the cliff.'

'What are you saying?' I feel odd and chilled.

Wiffy tips back his head and licks his lips.

'He's saying –' Sam comes into the hall.

'I'm not!' Wiffy runs at her. 'I'm not saying that, because *I* didn't do it! *You* –'

'Wiffy,' Christian steps forward. 'Shut your mouth!'

'Why should he?' Sam screams. 'Why must we always shut up?'

'Because –' Christian raises his hand, and I step between.

'You rat, Christian Owens!' I turn on him with anger that I never knew I had. 'Don't you *ever* do that again!'

I catch sight of the bus at the end of their street and I begin to run. I grab the rail as it's starting up, and although the conductor is grumbling about 'bloody kids', I scowl back at him, and hang on.

161

Sam's struggling to get her breath. As we make our way to the back seat, she coughs her vile, smoker's cough and I think she touches my arm. The bus starts unexpectedly. I look back guiltily and see Wiff, left behind, but Sam tells me not to bother. She's sick of him always tagging along. The bus swings round the corners and we laugh too loudly and cling on. Outside the town, the grassy slopes of the winding, high-banked lanes are shaded and silent and green.

At the stile, we jump down into the turf and follow the dusty path to the beach.

'I haven't been back,' Sam says, lighting a fag, 'or not much. In fact, I've hardly been back here at all.'

On the edges of the cliff, cushions of pink sea thrift are still in bloom.

'You know about the steps, though?'

'Oh yes. And about that stupid car, what went over the edge. Wiff told me that.'

The tide has turned and the pool at the base of the Red Rock is being covered up as the waves run in. Sam stops at the seat and we sit down. There's no one in sight.

'About my uncle,' she says at last, 'about that pig, Glyn –'

'Yes?'

No one is treading across the shifting bank of shingle and no one plays in the sand.

'It isn't what you think, Helen, it isn't like what people think at all.'

I look at her and I know that I don't understand.

'It was my Dad first, in secret and not often, just some-times, when we were left alone. Me and Wiff, both. The bastard didn't care. And I was afraid of my dad, Helen, always, and all the time. I was so scared of him, Helen, I used to –' She stops and sniffs. 'I was scared of him, like you were of that dog.'

Then, I see Tom again, taking off his shirt.

'And when my mum found out, she left. She didn't know what she could do. Not that I blame her, Helen, but I wish she hadn't gone away. Or that she'd come back.'

'Do you?'

'Oh yes,' she nods vigorously. 'You always do.'

I can see the edge where he had stood and the jaws of rock below.

'My mum was ashamed of me. That's what it was. She didn't think much of me, just like your Gran. And I know I shouldn't have done those things, and didn't ever want to either, or not with him, or Glyn. I don't think much of myself either, but they were filthy rotten beasts, the both of them. They were cruel to me. And Wiff.'

She pushes back her hair and looks down at the place where we had all stood. She smiles a bit and I realize that she can see Tom, too, in the distant summer sun.

'That's why I didn't reach out my hand, Helen. I know I should have. You and Tom would have tried to help, but I didn't. I didn't even try!'

'But you were a *kid*. It was an accident. We were *all* kids, you and I both. And Tom!'

'Not *that*, Helen!' She jumps up and shades her eyes again, and looks out to sea. 'That's not what I mean.'

'Aren't you talking about the Red Rock Dive, and how you pushed me, and how I fell in the sea? Aren't you talking about that day, and Tom?'

I remember the water in my mouth and the green-grey weight above.

'No! I'm not talking about *that*, Helen, though truthfully I wish I was.' As she turns back to me, I remember how Christian had stood on the cliffs and slowly scanned the sea.

'You're talking about the *Black Pig*, aren't you? And your

163

father, and what happened out there at sea.'

'Am I?' She laughs harshly, but she's not laughing at me. 'I suppose I am, aren't I? But then, I always was a silly bitch, or that's what people say. Especially in the shop. They call me a witch and a slut, and they ask if I'm having them on. But I'm not, Helen. I'm telling the truth to you.'

'They *know*, don't they? Both Christian and Wiffy. They've known, haven't they, all along.'

'Of course they have,' she whispers, 'but we promised, all three of us, not to tell. Only . . .'

'Only what?'

'Only it's *you*, coming back here, Helen, and being so kind, and me remembering Tom.'

'I haven't been *kind*, Sam.'

'You have, Helen, you've been kind to me, and I appreciate that a lot. But it's not just that. It's me, as well, remembering Tom.'

She drags in a great gust of breath and fixes her gaze on the high, hot edge of the Red Rock.

'My dad was drunk, that's what he was. Not particularly, not for my dad, but drunk all the same, and that day the sea was rough. Not very, but choppy-like, which it often is off the coast, so you need to take care and you need to hang on. Which he didn't. He stood up, Helen, sudden like, as though he'd thought of something, and then he let go. That's all he did. He stood up and slipped forward, with one foot caught for a moment, and then he went in. And I was the one beside him, because he liked that, having me near. So, I was the one who could have helped because Christian was checking the lines and Wiff was down below. And I saw his face there, in the water, just for a moment, and I didn't reach out. Not straight away. Not like your Tom did, for you. I knew the stupid, drunken sod couldn't

164

swim and just for that moment, I watched him there, in the water, before I began to shout. But when I did, and Wiff and Christian came, he was already gone.'

'That wasn't your fault, Sam.'

'Wasn't it?'

'No! No way! He was drunk and he fell in.'

'Glyn says it's my fault. And he's said he'll tell. That's why I sleep with him, Helen, that's why I have to keep on. That's what I wanted to explain this morning, only I didn't know how.'

'Glyn's lying to you, Sam. I know he is because I heard him in the pub. He accused your brother, then. It was drunken rubbish, so I didn't think about it again. It wasn't your fault.'

'Wasn't it, Helen? How can you be so sure?' She sits down and feels through her pockets again but doesn't find a fag.

'I'm sure, because –'

'Because? What is it Helen? You've gone as white as a ghost.'

So I tell her what I've never told anyone before.

It was evening, and the sun was low and dazzling. There's no dispute about that. It had been such a hot day and it seemed to me that we had been playing outside for ever, and always in the sun. I suppose we must have gone home for lunch because we usually did, but by the middle of the afternoon the metal sides of the slide had got so hot that they had scorched a sore, red mark on the outside of my leg. After that, I hadn't slid any more. I had wandered over to the sandpit and played there because it was under trees, and cooler, when you dug down.

Over on the freshly mown pitch, the older children were playing cricket. Some were still standing, but others were flopped out on their stomachs, their chins amongst the daisies in the grass. If a ball rolled near they sometimes stuck out a lazy arm. We'd had ice-cream, and then lollies, and the back of my neck felt stiff and tight with sun. I had sat on the edge of the sandpit, and licked, and then Tom had come over as well. He had said that he was bored with cricket, and that it was far too hot. He had taken off his shirt.

He had suggested building a sand city, something as good as Ancient Greece. He began to get all the younger children organized, and I was happy and proud. He said I could do walls because I was good at that, and I used the ice-cream spoon for the parapet along the top. He was working nearby and when someone flicked sand into his hair, he laughed, but I rushed over and brushed it off. I can remember that, and the strong smell of his skin, which was warm underneath.

We were nowhere near finished when it was time to go home. I fussed and cried and he promised that it wouldn't be spoilt over night. In the morning we could build together again. I must have fussed even more, because he got me to march, like a Roman soldier, he said. He shouted, 'Left, left, left', and I marched and laughed all round the edge of the recreation ground.

He shouted, 'Halt!' at the kerbside and put his hand on my hot, burnt neck. I squirmed away. I wanted to do another step. I looked down at our feet, side by side, and mine so small, and although he'd said 'halt', I hadn't thought it mattered if I took another step. I swung my leg out for the stride ahead.

No one knew how Tom did it. All the witnesses agreed. And the van driver had been dazzled, that's why he was going so slowly, that's why he was taking care. He had his own young sons at home, and never recovered. He never drove or worked again. I learnt that later, because Dad occasionally met him in the pub.

Tom had pushed me aside, then lost his balance because he had moved so fast. He couldn't step back. That's all it was. That's what everybody said.

I never saw him in the air. Other people had seen that. I'd just run after, amazed that he'd disappeared. I'd knelt down on the softened tarmac and looked underneath. I could just reach his ankle and I'd tried to pull, or shake it a bit, to get him up or to make him crawl out. 'Tom,' I'd called but he hadn't answered me. He never even moved.

I stood up in the gutter, where his dropped shirt was, and I saw that there was blood on my legs. I thought I had hurt myself, so I began to cry.

'It's like fish isn't it?' she says. 'The slippery bastards. Why do they have to go and die?'